ALI SPARKES

NIGHT WALKER

OXFORD

UNIVERSITY PRESS

For Vicky, Ellie, Cameron, Kirsty &
Richard Maguire—an especially
warm-blooded clan.

OXFORD
UNIVERSITY PRESS

Great Clarendon Street, Oxford OX2 6DP

Oxford University Press is a department of the University of Oxford.
It furthers the University's objective of excellence in research, scholarship,
and education by publishing worldwide. Oxford is a registered trade mark of
Oxford University Press in the UK and in certain other countries

British Library Cataloguing in Publication Data
Data available

ISBN: 978-0-19-274997-0

1 3 5 7 9 10 8 6 4 2

Printed in Great Britain

Paper used in the production of this book is a natural,
recyclable product made from wood grown in sustainable forests.
The manufacturing process conforms to the environmental
regulations of the country of origin.

CHAPTER 1

SEVEN YEARS AGO

Nobody really knew who Cris Taylor was until the day he started screaming on the bus.

A thin, pale boy, he'd never said much. Dyslexia prevented him from ever shining in class and dyspraxia meant he would never excel in sports. Teachers at Harcourt Primary usually spelt his name with an H and sometimes forgot he was in the room.

Ask any one of them to describe Cris Taylor and they'd have to pause and wrinkle their brow. A bit skinny . . . ? Fair hair . . . ?

Until that day on the bus. After that day on the bus *everyone* remembered Cris Taylor.

It was a hot, sunny Friday—perfect for a school trip to *The World Gardens*. Everyone in his class seemed to be having a good time. Not an *amazing* time. Not many of them were seriously interested in the collection of plants and trees from all over the planet. Several had complained that there were no animals.

'What's the point of a flippin' monkey puzzle tree if it hasn't got monkeys up it?' whined Kyle Ryman, repeatedly thwacking his Spider-Man lunchbox against the trunk of the 15-metre-high evergreen until Mr Crosby threatened to send him back to the coach to sit on his own.

Cris shuddered. The coach was meant to have air conditioning but it wasn't working. Driving there it had been OK with the windows open—but sitting inside the coach in this heat would be unbearable. Kyle would probably melt. They'd go back at 2.30 p.m. and discover an empty uniform and a puddle of skin, bone, fat, and entrails slipping along under the seats.

'You all right?' Catriona Wild asked him. She was nice, Catriona. She had brown hair and blue eyes and uncountable freckles. Catriona always got plenty of attention—and she didn't really want it. Maybe that's why she liked him. Hanging out with Cris was like wearing a cloaking device. He was so unremarkable he sucked anybody into his field of unremarkableness like a black hole.

'I'm . . . a bit hot,' he said, as they traipsed out of the temperate house and along the path to the steamy glass of the rainforest zone. He didn't share his notion of Kyle's

2

melting skin and guts. He had a lot of weird, dark thoughts like this. People didn't always react well to them when he shared.

'You do look quite pink,' she said.

He didn't feel pink. He felt red raw. His skin was prickling and sore. He had put on extra sun cream twice since getting off the coach but it didn't seem to be helping.

Abruptly he veered away from the main party and over to the patch of darkness beneath a vast spreading cedar tree. 'Cris!' Catriona ran after him. 'We're meant to stay together! You'll get in trouble.'

But Cris didn't care about the rules. He was desperate to reach the dimness beneath the canopy. If he had to spend another five seconds in the sun he was going to spontaneously combust.

He flung himself onto the soft brown needly soil with a gasp of relief and lay with his head against one of the gnarly tree roots, panting like a dog. The pain was still tingling through him but the panic that went with it seemed to subside in the gloom. Catriona was an uneasy silhouette at the edge of the shadow, glancing back over her shoulder. 'We're not meant to go off on our own!' she insisted. 'It's not allowed!'

'I don't care,' he puffed. 'I'm not going anywhere. My skin hurts too much.'

Concerned, she stepped across and crouched down next to him, squinting at his arms. 'You're all veiny,' she said. 'Does your head ache? Maybe you've got heatstroke.'

'Maybe,' breathed Cris. He closed his eyes. There was a growing panic in the pit of his belly about having to leave this oasis. The pain was still really bad but in the shade he could just about keep his head. He could just about control himself. He knew Catriona was right; they would both get into trouble if they didn't get up now and run back to the main group as it headed into the rainforest zone.

But he couldn't do it. He just couldn't do it. Right now he felt like he was face to face with a bonfire. Stepping out of this shade would be like throwing himself on top of it.

'TAYLOR!'

He jumped violently and Catriona gave a little squeak.

'WILD!'

It could only be Mr Crosby. No other teacher called Year 6s by their surnames. He was like some kind of cartoon teacher from a comic strip. Sometimes he even shook his fist and went 'Grrrr!'.

'Get over here, NOW!'

Catriona ran, hissing: 'I told you!'

But Cris only got as far as the edge of the shade. He stood, shaking and sweating, and put his forearm out into the sunlight. Instantly the burning was worse than ever. He yelped and snatched his arm back into the shade. Mr Crosby was striding over now, looking thunderous behind his thin, steel-framed glasses.

'TAYLOR! What do you think you're doing? I just told you to GET BACK OVER HERE!'

'Sir . . . I can't,' said Cris. 'It . . . it hurts.'

'What are you talking about?!' Mr Crosby reached the tree, his pale blue shirt see-through with sweat, and beads of perspiration clinging to his balding head.

'It's too hot,' said Cris. 'It burns my skin.'

'Oh for heaven's sake—we're all hot, boy! Did you put sun cream on?'

'Yes, sir—three times,' said Cris, holding out his arms which were slick with white smears of Factor 50.

'And you've got a hat on, so stop making such a fuss,' said Mr Crosby. 'A bit of sun isn't going to kill you.'

'But . . .'

'Enough! Come on. NOW.' Mr Crosby turned and walked back to the others and there was no doubt he expected to be followed.

Cris took a deep breath, pulled the peak on his cap down low, and ran. Running was the only option. Staying still was far, far worse. Even so, it felt as if the blue, cloudless sky was raining needles. He overtook the teacher and caught up with Catriona as she followed the rest of the class into the rainforest zone. He staggered into the tall glass temple of greenery and under the massive leaf of an umbrella plant, gulping in the heavy, moist air and trying not to whimper.

For the next ten minutes he slipped quickly from specimen to specimen, darting across any daggers of sunshine that made it past the leaves. The pain was still awful but the panic wound down a bit. He could manage it. If he just stayed in the shade he could manage. And then it was lunchtime.

'OK, everyone—we're going outside for sandwiches now,' said Miss Barnes. 'Please stay together in the picnic area.'

The picnic area had wooden bench tables and seats and a green carpet of grass. And not one tree. Cris felt sick. The nearest shade did not reach even a finger into the glaring sunlight that washed their lunch spot. He took another deep breath as he exited the rainforest zone. It felt as if he'd stepped into the Sahara desert. Seconds later he was running again—straight for the nearest tree, a good ten metres beyond the picnic park, fear pounding through him and driving the pain up to fever pitch.

Mr Crosby caught up with him before he could get out his sandwiches. He spoke through tight lips that barely moved. 'Get yourself BACK to the others, Taylor! NOW!'

'Sir . . . Please . . . I won't go anywhere else. Can I just stay here for a little while? Please?'

'No, Taylor—you canNOT. I won't tell you again. Get back to the others. And don't give me any more reason to talk to you, you understand?'

Cris joined the others. He didn't eat much lunch. The pain was now so great it was flashing across his skin in scalding, rolling waves. Tears were seeping out of his eyes, but he kept his head down and the peak of his cap hid his face. Catriona had gone to join Rebecca Marsh and so didn't check him out. He was quite glad of that. He needed to concentrate on not whimpering out loud.

By the time they all got back on the coach he was breathing in shallow gasps again, like an exhausted dog. He found a seat on the shady side and huddled into it, wincing as his bare arm touched the warm glass of the window. He tried to take deep breaths and calm himself, the way his mum had taught him whenever he'd felt panicky. Long—slow—breaths. Keep—calm. It—will—pass . . .

The air conditioning on the vehicle coughed into life and cooled them all down a bit and this probably helped him survive just a little longer, breathing deep and slow with his eyes closed. A cold air nozzle just above his head took the agony down perhaps as much as three per cent. Then the coach drew up outside Harcourt Primary and the driver switched off the engine—and the aircon—as soon as he'd parked. It was just after the end of school and the parents of the kids who'd gone on the trip were all waiting at the gates. Cris couldn't wait to run to Mum and beg her to get him into her shady, cool Renault and take him home.

But Mr Crosby was at the front of the coach, by the open door, and sending the kids out one by one to their parents, working through their names in alphabetical order. 'STAY IN YOUR SEATS!' he bellowed at Kyle Ryman and Ben Jenkins as they grabbed their bags and bundled into the aisle. They sat down, rolling their eyes and muttering swear words.

Cris stayed where he was too. Hemmed in by Jonas Lane.

In a shaft of warm golden sun. With no more cool air nozzle.

It was inescapable. He began to sink down in his seat and slide into the footwell, whimpering audibly now, so that Jonas turned and stared at him. And Mr Crosby was still only on H—holding each child back on the step of the coach until a parent or guardian came forward to collect them. Still a dozen letters away from release, Cris felt himself burst into flame.

A scream erupted from his throat. It sounded terrifying. Another followed it. And then another.

Mr Crosby dropped his clipboard.

Cris didn't remember much about it later. A flurry of activity; someone pressing him down onto the seat, his face full in sun, checking his pulse and yelling for the first aid box. Then Mum—thank god—Mum—was there and pulling everyone off him and gathering him up, throwing her jacket over him and carrying him off the bus and away to the car and its tinted glass.

Then home to a darkened room. Then cool cucumber pads on his skin and an antihistamine tablet and water and the fan on full and then sleep, sleep, dark, dark, sleep.

But not before he heard her whisper: 'I'm so sorry. I'm so, so sorry.'

Which was when he understood.

It came from her.

CHAPTER 2

NOW

Spin lay on his back, arms folded across his chest, like a recently laid out corpse. Only his open eyes, blinking occasionally in the gloom, gave away that he was still alive.

Above him dangled blood. Blood in bags. Rather a lot of it. One of the bags was ruby red. The other was so dark maroon it was nearly black.

'Hey, man,' said the boy in the next bed. 'I 'ope that black stuff's what came out . . . not what's going in.'

Spin sighed and turned his head. 'Surely it's time they came back and screwed you over again,' he said.

The boy gave him a sour look. 'Yeah, thanks for reminding me, Dracula.'

If he thought *that* was getting a reaction, he thought wrong. Spin just smiled and turned his gaze back up to the bags of blood. It would be hours, yet, before the new stuff was fully in. Literally every bad cell was being drained from his veins and replaced by the shiny red happy cells donated by normal people.

He would be here another twenty-four hours; time enough to hear old Metal Leg get into his full opera of screaming behind the cubicle curtain at least twice more. The boy's name was Alistair and he'd been born with a club foot. The muscles in his right leg were constantly tugging his bones into some kind of grim helter-skelter shape. Every few months he needed to come into hospital to be fitted into a metal cage of wires and screws. To encourage his leg to stop its misbehaviour, the screws had to be regularly hand turned, by an orthopaedic specialist. At the point Spin had arrived on the ward Alistair had been howling with agony behind the curtain—his first screw twist of the day. He explained why about half an hour later when the meds had kicked in and he was able to talk.

It was rare to meet someone who knew as much about pain as he did and Spin did not underestimate the boy's suffering. But there was a good chance the suffering would end one day— either in success from all the screw twisting or in amputation. Alistair was more than ready for the lopping it off option. These days, amputees could get cool running blades and enter the Olympics.

There were no such career opportunities for a boy like Spin. And no real end in sight to his condition.

Vampire.

Hmmm. Who would have thought there would ever be a treatment for that? And yet all those red blood cells, gleaming down at him from the bags, running into him through a tube, were freely given. What came out of him, sticky and dark, was freely given too. He didn't want it.

'So . . . if you step out in the sun . . .' Alistair had started up again, laying aside his luridly bright wrestling magazine. '. . .will you shrivel up and die?'

'Yes,' said Spin, keeping his eyes on the bags.

'And, like, do you need human blood to survive?'

'We all need human blood to survive,' replied Spin. He got up on one elbow and grinned across at Alistair, allowing his sharply pointed canine teeth to twinkle out below his upper lip. 'Or are you offering?'

Alistair picked up his magazine again and buried his head in it. Spin heard him mutter: 'Freak.' He chose not to respond further. The blood exchange was rather taking it out of him. Two intravenous lines ran up his thigh and went straight into his femoral vein; one for *in* and one for *out*. It hurt. And itched. Pinned him to this bed for hours. He was forced to pee in a bedpan. If erythropoietic protoporphyria didn't kill you, the humiliation might.

They'd tried to get the exchange moving in and out through veins in his arms but nothing doing. His body didn't want to give up its own weird liquid that passed for blood. His arm veins refused to co-operate until the line team decided to go in with the femoral lines. Not much will stop blood traffic through a femoral vein.

11

The light bouncing off the polished ward floor was messing with him. Not hurting exactly but tickling. They'd covered his bed with a sort of black gazebo and switched off the lights above it. Energy-saving bulbs and fluorescent strips were everywhere in this hospital. These were almost as bad as the sun. He closed his eyes and breathed deeply. Sleep would be good.

One bed away from Cage Fighter was a red-haired girl with some kind of heart problem. She lay quietly, drifting in and out of sleep, a monitor beeping out her life signs and oxygen funnelling into her nostrils through a forked plastic tube. Younger than Elena, he reckoned . . . but maybe older than Tima. Probably about twelve. He'd been in here two days and so had she. In that time the girl had seen no visitor other than a distracted female social worker who plonked a magazine and a bunch of aged-looking grapes on the girl's bedside table around lunchtime yesterday, played with her phone for ten minutes, and then departed.

Nobody else since then, other than doctors. No *Get Well Soon* cards on her bedside table either.

No family, he deduced. Bad luck.

His blood pressure took a dive at this point, sounding an alarm on his own monitor. He sank down into a state so limp and lost, that his last thought was that his atoms had simply given up holding him in a physical shape and he was dissolving into the mattress.

But no. Hello. He was back again. They'd stabilized him. Cage Fighter was staring across, agog, as the team checked Spin's blood pressure again and again. And then the red-haired girl's monitor started to shriek and they all ran to see to her instead.

It was quite an entertaining afternoon for Cage Fighter. It ended badly for the red-haired girl though.

She died.

CHAPTER 3

'Sir! Sir! He's bleeding, sir!'

Mr Makepeace strode across the gym, swiping a sports towel off the benches, looking weary rather than concerned. Matt leant against the climbing bars and pinched the bridge of his nose to stop the flow. He would rather have dealt with this himself. If Ahmed was trying to be helpful, he could do without that kind of help. Especially from Ahmed who was a first-class loser.

'What have you done to yourself, Wheeler?' sighed Mr Makepeace.

'Nothing,' burbled Matt, despite the very clear evidence that it was definitely something. He accepted the towel and pressed it to his nostrils.

The sports teacher glanced around at sixty boys leaping, running, and skidding, trainers squeaking, across the varnished tiled floor; some playing basketball, others on circuit training. 'Ball in the face, was it?' he said, searching for a guilty party on the basketball court and finding no takers.

'Not sure,' grunted Matt, through the towel. 'I didn't see.'

Mr Makepeace folded his arms, looking sceptical. 'So— you're bleeding all over my gym floor and you have no idea why. That's what you're telling me?'

Again, he looked around and again, nothing. He missed the smirk from Liam Bassiter and the slight red mark on the boy's forehead. Liam had been quick about it—and clever, Matt had to admit. Waiting until Matt was just behind him on the circuit, heading for the climbing bars, Liam had ducked down to tie a lace and then abruptly twisted round and whacked his forehead into Matt's face in a way that could almost have been an accident . . . except for the gleam in his enemy's eyes and the words under his breath: 'No help for you in here, Feathers.'

Pain had splintered up through his nose like a firework and blood spurted out a second later.

The bleeding had stopped by the time he and Mr Makepeace reached the sink in the changing room. Matt wedged some tissue up his nose and told the teacher he was sure it wasn't broken. He wasn't completely sure, but he really didn't want to spend his lunch hour sitting in the medical area behind reception.

'I'm fide,' he told Mr Makepeace. 'I'll dust sid dowd od da bench for a liddle bid.'

The teacher nodded and left Matt to sit, bloody towel in hand, while his wounded nostrils coagulated. Matt could handle

15

the ache, the metallic taste in his throat and the unpleasant sensation of thick clotting as he breathed carefully through his mouth. That was no big deal. But the anger in him was. It was bubbling like lava. The urge to go after Liam and slam his face into the vaulting horse was so strong he was shaking with it.

Liam looked right across at him, that smirk back across his narrow, mean face. He made a little flapping action with his hands, shook his head and affected a sad expression. *No help from the birdies!* he mouthed.

Matt glanced up at the high windows. All twelve of them framed a clear blue winter sky, and only one of these views had a bird in it. The small black shape fluttered briefly against the glass. Matt shook his head and the shape took flight and vanished.

Liam was getting up from a forward roll but he still managed to follow Matt's eyeline and see the brief exchange between boy and bird. His face flickered for just a moment, losing composure. Then he shook his head and pasted the smirk back on, rubbing his hands through his sweaty, dark red buzz cut and stalking away to the parallel bars. Liam loved the parallel bars. His upper body strength was impressive. They'd had several fights now and Matt knew Liam could throw a meaningful punch with those muscles. Liam executed several chin-ups, lifting his whole bodyweight until his chin rose above the bar. Then he dropped to the mat and turned to look at Matt again, flexing his pecs.

Matt snorted. A mistake. The fragile clot in his nose gave way and blood streamed down his face again. This time Mr

Makepeace sent him to reception. 'Don't bleed on the corridor floors,' he said. 'It's a slip hazard.'

'Thanks, sir,' muttered Matt. 'I'm touched.'

But Mr Makepeace had no known sense of humour and just turned back to the gym with a groan as shouting suddenly erupted among the boys on his watch. 'What now?' he sighed.

The receptionist was more sympathetic and settled him in an easy chair with an ice pack and instructions to sit quietly for half an hour. Tiredness began to take hold of him, as it often did by the afternoon, and he closed his eyes and started drifting off, lulled by the gentle clicks of the receptionist at her monitor and keyboard.

He'd probably had about four hours' sleep last night. Since the clocks had gone back to Greenwich Mean Time he—and Elena and Tima—had all been suffering. It's not easy being an insomniac with an unnerving habit of waking up at precisely the same time every night. But he and his mates in the Wide Awake Club hadn't thought for a moment that their sleeping hours could get even shorter. During British Summer Time some kind of cosmic beam shot through Thornleigh, waking all three of them at precisely 1.34 a.m. and after that they were lucky to snatch an hour or two more before breakfast.

But now, in Greenwich Mean Time, that beam came through just exactly as it had the night before. Only, thanks to light saving adjustments across the British Isles, it was now snapping them awake at *12*.34 a.m.

Brilliant.

'You look like I feel,' said a familiar voice.

Matt snapped awake. The receptionist was further down the office, on the phone, and Elena was filling out a form on the counter, her wheat-coloured hair falling across her face as she scribbled on the paper. He knew that underneath that curtain her blue eyes were shadowed with exhaustion.

'I bet you don't feel like this.' He lifted the towel to reveal his messed up nose. His fellow insomniac winced.

'What happened?'

'Liam Bassiter head-butted me in the gym,' he said, keeping his voice low.

Elena shook back her hair, frowning. 'He just won't leave you alone, will he? He's going to get himself expelled. Just . . . make sure he doesn't take you with him.'

Matt rolled his eyes. 'It was a stealth head-butt. Nobody saw.'

She raised an eyebrow. 'And you're not telling.'

'Nope.' Matt tenderly touched the bridge of his nose. It was puffy but the bleeding seemed to have stopped properly now. 'I'll get back at him in my own way.'

Elena's eyes flickered to the window. 'You know you can't—'

'I don't mean that,' snapped Matt. 'I'm not stupid. I'm not doing that again.'

Elena breathed out. 'Good. Although . . .' she suppressed a grin, ' . . . it would be good to see it. Liam Bassiter, pecked unconscious.' She shook her head, smile fading. 'But you know what they say about superpowers.'

'Yeah, yeah, spare me the Spider-Man speech,' said Matt. 'I'll find another way to get even with that lump of—'

'Sharon! Call 999!' Mrs Grace ran into reception looking anxious. 'And get all the first aiders to the gym.'

Sharon was already dialling and calling out: 'What's happened?'

'We don't know for sure,' called Mrs Grace, running back down the corridor. 'Liam Bassiter's just collapsed.'

CHAPTER 4

'Tima! Where are you and what are you doing?'

Spencer turned his eyes on her and they both agreed he should probably make himself scarce.

'Mum won't be happy if she finds you here,' said Tima.

'TIMA! Do I have to come up there and get you?!' yelled Mum.

'NOOOO—I'll be down in a minute!' she called back. She didn't want to let Spencer go. She'd got closer to him than she could ever have imagined. She would never have believed this could happen just a few months ago.

The door crashed open and Mum stood there. Spencer froze. Mum froze. Spencer legged it across the carpet. Mum tried to kill him.

'MUM! NOOOOO!' shrieked Tima, throwing herself

between them.

Mum would have ended Spencer, Tima had no doubt, but she was too late to catch him. Instead she turned and stared at her daughter, slowly shaking her head.

Tima got up from the carpet and shoved her hands deep into her jeans pockets. She looked around the room at her posters ... Darcey Bussell, Adele, Francesca Hayward, Ella Fitzgerald, Maddie Ziegler; stars of dance and song, all around her walls. Baby ballet shoes pinned up above her bed. Pink lampshade and purple duvet cover. Ballerina Barbie on the shelf. She had to admit, even to herself, that this room didn't match who she had become.

'Mum,' she muttered. 'It's not how it looks.' She glimpsed one of Spencer's legs behind the radiator and willed him to stay put.

Mum shook her head. 'You're alone in your room ... playing with a spider. How is that not how it looks?'

'His name is Spencer,' said Tima, flopping back down on her bed. 'And he's not just any spider. He's ... my friend.'

Mum briefly closed her eyes. 'Tima ... I know you've got this ... thing about insects. And that's fine.'

'Spencer's not an insect; he's an—'

'Arachnid! Yes, I know!' snapped Mum. 'I didn't spend seven years studying to be a vet without working out what animal group a spider belongs to!'

Tima folded her arms and said nothing.

'I just think ... you should be making friends with *people*,' said Mum. She sat down on the bed next to Tima and took her hand. 'I mean . . . girls from school, maybe.'

Tima winced. She didn't have a friend at school . . . not a real one. And she didn't really want one. 'I *have* got a friend,' she said. 'Elena is my friend.'

'Yes, I know,' said Mum, 'and she's lovely. But she's a bit older than you and she's not at your school and . . .'

'OK, Mum—I get it.' Tima stood up and grabbed her phone and her sparkly cardi off the chair. 'You'd like me to have a nice *posh* friend from my nice *posh* school.'

Mum stared up at her, looking wounded, and Tima felt guilty. She knew this wasn't what Mum meant, but it was a way of changing the subject. 'You know that's not what I mean,' said Mum, reading her mind. 'I just want to you spend less time in your room, talking to . . . arachnids . . . and more time having a social life with girls your own age. Or boys! I don't mind boys . . . although your dad probably will.'

'It's fine, Mum,' said Tima. 'I know I'm weird. But I'm trying not to be. That's why we're going to Lily's paaaarteeee.' She rolled her eyes and, happily, Mum lightened up and laughed, following her out across the landing and down the stairs.

'You said yourself you need to try to get on better with her,' Mum said, as they put on their coats and picked up the prettily-wrapped birthday present and card. 'You both sing so beautifully together. And now you both get asked to do all these shows . . . well . . . you have to be—'

'—professional. Yes I know. So take me to Lily's party and I'll show you how professional I can be,' said Tima.

Mum pulled the front door shut and strode towards the Land Rover, peering across at her daughter. 'Are you really only eleven?' she said. 'Sometimes you sound just like my older sister!' They got in, shut the doors and belted up. 'You really should just . . . be eleven,' Mum went on. 'Have fun. Don't take life so seriously.'

'I do have fun,' Tima said. 'It's just that sometimes I have to save the planet.'

Mum laughed. So did Tima. Although she was being factual, not fanciful. In the past few months she, Elena, and Matt, together with her insect and arachnid buddies, had saved at least the town of Thornleigh and very possibly the planet too—twice. Sometimes the urge to tell all of it to Mum was so strong . . . but there was no way she could. No way. She imagined it sometimes, especially when she was lying awake in the dark.

'Mum, Dad,' she would say, sitting them down at the kitchen table, 'I know you're going to find this hard to believe . . . but I have a kind of . . . superpower.' They would smile at her indulgently and cast their eyes upwards, chuckling, wondering what game she was playing. Then she'd say: 'No . . . really. You know this thing I have about insects and spiders . . . it's not just an "interest" . . . it's a superpower. I can speak to them. And they can speak to me. I ask them to do things for me and . . . they do.' Then she would lift her hands and blow across her palms and two hundred butterflies and moths would funnel in through the skylight and stage an aerobatic display across the ceiling. Mum and Dad would sit and watch, their mouths falling open, as the insects curled and spun like circus performers, twisting and fluttering in ribbons of colour, before finishing with a hovering formation, spelling out

HELLO, TIMA'S MUM AND DAD!

Then there would be an amazed silence and she would say: 'I've been able to do this since May . . . since the time I started waking up at 1.34 a.m. . . . and met Elena and Matt out in the dark because I couldn't bear to stay alone in my room every night. It's why I've got so weird . . . and . . . by the way . . . we've all saved the planet. Twice.'

Trouble was, she couldn't imagine anything happening next which could be a good thing.

'Well, you're dressed like you're going to have fun anyway,' said Mum as they pulled out of the drive and onto the road. 'You look lovely.'

Tima glanced down. She was wearing a red tunic with matching red tights and shiny patent leather red boots, her black sparkly cardi on top and her long dark hair up in a high ponytail. Party wear! These days she was more at home in her stretchy black jeans, sweatshirt and black jazz shoes . . . her 'cat burglar' look as Elena called it. When they hung out in the dark she could be almost invisible in it. But it was nice to dress up for a party . . . even if it was Lily Fry's party. And it was nice that Lily had asked her. A few months ago that would never have happened. It was amazing what music could do to bring people together.

They might not really like each other but when they sang together at school it sounded pretty amazing. Lily obviously thought it was worth making an effort . . . so fair enough.

The party was rolling nicely by the time they arrived at Lily's impressive house. It was large, with high brick walls around it, a sweeping drive up to the balloon-festooned front door. In the hallway a sparkling crystal chandelier dangled high over a black and white tiled floor. A massive framed portrait of Lily, looking much younger and impossibly cute, hung halfway up the elegantly curved staircase.

'TIMA!' Lily rushed through the hall with her best friends, Clara and Keira, in her wake. She flung her arms around Tima in a theatrical way. Her blonde hair was laced with tiny crystal stars, matching the stars twinkling on her pink dress. She looked perfect . . . like an expensive doll. 'I'm so glad you could come! Oh—thank you!' She took the present and the card and ran to put it with the others, piled high across an ornate marble-topped hallway table. 'Mummy says I must wait until after tea to open them,' she said. 'Come along! The entertainer is about to start, and then we've got a piñata and then tea . . .'

Tima glanced back at Mum who was chatting to Lily's mother by the front door. 'Go on!' Mum said, waving her away.

The entertainer wasn't quite what Tima had expected. She'd pictured a magician with a top hat, pulling out rabbits, or maybe a puppeteer, tucked into a corner of the living room. In fact the whole living room—which was the size of two or three normal people's living rooms—was transformed into a theatre, with seats set in rows and swooping silk curtains hung across one end of it. There was even stage lighting on poles—and a small sound and lighting desk positioned at the back of the room.

Tima sat down a row behind Lily, amid about forty other kids who seemed to be a mixture of school friends and family. The curtains began to open, humming across on their tracks by remote control, and then, as the audience fell into an excited hush, the music started. It was the theme to *The Lion King*. There was a sudden blaze of light as the curtains revealed the stage, and the 'entertainer' stepped forward . . . dressed and made up to look exactly like Simba from *The Lion King* stage show. Tima's jaw dropped as he went into *The Circle of Life* in front of an amazing painted backdrop of trees and grasses and animals. Halfway through the song he was joined by two female singers and dancers, also in full costume as young lionesses.

Tima heard one of the mums whispering: 'Yes . . . from the West End show. She hired them and paid their travel expenses. Amazing!'

Tima blinked at the back of Lily's perfect, starry blonde head. It was true. Her mother had literally brought three of the actual cast of *The Lion King* to East Anglia on a Sunday afternoon, to perform excerpts of the show for her daughter's eleventh birthday party. What would she do for her twelfth? Build a rink and stage *Cinderella on Ice* in the back garden?

The show went on for half an hour and was amazing. Afterwards the cast posed for photos with everybody. Tima would have loved to talk to the performers about how they got started but there wasn't time because now everybody had to go outside and leap about, bashing sticks at a life-sized paper donkey hung from a tree. Every so often the bashing would produce a shower of sweets as the piñata's papery hide split open. There was a lot of shrieking and grunting. Kind of violent for such a *nice* party, Tima thought. She wandered away back to the house and found Mum chatting to Keira's mother near the party food.

'. . .how I'm going to top this when Keira turns eleven,' Keira's mum was muttering. 'I mean! It's . . . amazing, but . . .'

'Makes you feel a bit inadequate, doesn't it?' Mum said, quietly. 'I used to think pass-the-parcel was excitement enough . . .'

'It's the party bags I'm terrified of,' said Keira's mum. 'I don't think it'll be a balloon, a whistle, and a bit of cake, do you?'

'No. Probably a Gucci watch, truffles, and a Fabergé egg,' giggled Mum. 'Top that.'

As incredible as Lily's party was, one kid went home early. A thin, pale girl came through, saying she felt sick. Lily's mum swept her away into the hallway and phoned for someone to come and get her. 'I think it's all a bit too much for her,' Tima heard Mrs Fry say.

Tima leant on the wall near the door, peering through at the girl. She didn't seem to fit in, here in this beautiful, expensive house. Her pale blue dress was a bit worn and her party shoes weren't shiny. Her auburn hair was in untidy plaits. None of the other kids had spoken to her as far as Tima was aware. She hung her head and scuffed her feet back and forth on the black and white tiles while Mrs Fry went to fetch her party bag.

'Are you OK?' asked Tima, stepping across the hallway.

27

The girl looked up and shrugged. 'Just tired,' she said. 'And a bit dizzy.' There were shadows under her brown eyes.

'Do you . . . do you have trouble sleeping?' asked Tima, her pulse picking up.

'No,' said the girl. 'I sleep too much. Always gettin' told to get up and stop bein' lazy these days.'

'Oh. How long have you been feeling . . . tired?'

She shrugged again. 'I dunno. Two weeks . . . three?'

Mrs Fry came back with a large pink paper bag full of party goodies. She patted the girl on the head. 'I hope you enjoy them, Megan,' she said in a clipped voice. Then the bell rang. 'That's your taxi now. Will you be all right going back to the home on your own? The staff are expecting you.'

Megan nodded. She gave a wan smile to Tima and then ambled off to her taxi, clutching the party bag to her chest. Mrs Fry waved and closed the door. She turned, noticed Tima, and smiled an exact replica of Lily's smile; a little tight. 'Poor Megan,' she said. 'She's one of the children I sponsor at a care home. I think all this . . .' she waved a beautifully manicured hand, 'is a bit overwhelming for her.'

Tima was about to say: 'It's overwhelming for *me*!' but she stopped herself.

'Is she one of Lily's friends?' she asked.

'Oh no,' said Mrs Fry. 'Lily wouldn't . . . I mean . . . they don't really move in the same circles. I just like to do my bit from time to time and offer a needy child a place at a lovely party. Make them feel a bit special.'

Special? pondered Tima. In a 'totally ignored by all the other kids' kind of way . . . ? She couldn't help thinking it was Mrs Fry who wanted to feel special. In a saintly kind of way.

'Come along, Tima,' said Mrs Fry, her smile getting a bit higher on her very smooth face. 'It's time for—OH MY GOD!'

Mrs Fry flung her hands up to her mouth. Through her fingers she breathed: 'Don't move . . . don't . . . move.'

Tima looked behind her, half expecting to see an escaped tiger—perhaps from a surprise zoo that had been hidden around the side of the house for after tea—getting ready to pounce. But there was nothing there.

When she looked back again, Mrs Fry was advancing on her with a rolled-up magazine, revulsion on her face. 'It's . . . on your shoulder. Just . . . keep still!'

It was then Tima realized that Spencer had come along to the party with her. He must have jumped into her sparkly cardigan and hidden under the collar. He was now sitting on her shoulder like a big, black, hairy-legged brooch. Then she realized the rolled-up magazine was swooshing down towards him.

'NO!' Tima threw out both hands and deflected the magazine with such force that Mrs Fry screamed, jolted, and toppled over backwards on her high heels. She dropped the magazine as she went, and scrabbled wildly at the edge of the marble table, provoking an avalanche of beautifully-wrapped presents and cards. Seconds later she lay groaning beneath her daughter's bashed and dented parcels just as Lily, Clara, Keira, and assorted other kids and mums came running into the hallway to see what had happened.

Tima stood as still as rock while Spencer just sat there,

staring with all eight eyes, at the spectacle he had caused. She got the distinct impression he was as close to laughing as an invertebrate ever got.

Lily, though, was enraged. She stared at her mother and her messy pile of gifts and cards, and then up at Tima with eyes full of fury and accusation. Eventually she broke the silence with a trembling voice. 'Tima . . . you always have to ruin *everything*!' She gave a sob, turned, and stormed up the stairs with Keira and Clara running after her, cooing with sympathy.

Tima didn't stay for the party bag.

CHAPTER 5

Elena kept perfectly still. She could feel the beast getting closer; sense its beating heart. In the gloom she saw a flash of its sharp teeth and then, before she could even cry out, it was upon her.

Elena put up her hands and squeezed its furry head. A delighted laugh spilled out of her as she pulled the fox into a hug. It was an incredible privilege to get this close to a wild animal and even though she and Velma had been friends for a few months now, she had never presumed, never expected the vixen to allow her to pet it like a dog.

But in the last couple of weeks Velma had become totally relaxed with her. Maybe it was because her cubs were nearly independent now. She had more time to develop this strange bond with a human girl. She didn't follow Elena around like Lucky followed Matt. But it was easier for Lucky; she could roost on Matt's bedroom windowsill, or above him, on the edge of the forecourt canopy, when he was working at the family car wash. Most people didn't notice his feathered friend. A fox would draw more attention.

'Come on,' Elena said, getting to her feet. 'It's too cold to sit around. I'm going to the hide. You want to come?'

Velma trotted along with her to the edge of the trees under the railway arch. Occasionally, Elena marvelled at how comfortable a teenage girl could be out in the dark. Her eyesight adjusted to it very quickly these days and she only used her torch deep in the trees. Of course, it helped that hundreds of friends were sharing the night with her. She sensed them all around her, from the mice, shrews, and voles in the grass to the squirrels in the trees. The foxes and badgers were easy with her walks through their world; they didn't vanish as soon as they saw her but often stood, raised their heads, and watched her pass. Only Velma routinely greeted her and walked with her, but Elena also had squirrel friends who occasionally clambered up her legs or dropped onto her shoulders.

Velma paused beneath a tall silver birch tree. Elena paused too. The sky had suddenly lit up with a bright green flare. The flash was gone almost as soon as it arrived. Fox and girl stared at each other. 'It's just a firework,' said Elena. 'Left over from Guy Fawkes Night.' She didn't hear a bang, though. Velma flicked her ears and then slid away into the shadows, distracted by something she wanted to hunt. Elena waved her off, happily, knowing they'd be in each other's company again soon.

Tima was already at the hide when she got to it. The

wooden hut was built high in a cluster of trees, with a metal ladder reaching up to it. Although they'd done a lot to improve the hut inside, outside they'd been careful to leave it as close to how they'd found it as possible. The ladder was engulfed with ivy in places and they had to be careful not to slip or trip on it as they climbed. The ivy was good camouflage; they didn't want anyone else to spot the ladder and discover their den.

Tima was sitting on a beanbag, next to the battery-powered lantern which rested on a small trunk. She appeared to be deep in conversation with a spider.

'Hey! Spencer's come out for the night!' said Elena, grinning.

'Hmmmm,' said Tima, as the arachnid wandered across her knuckles. 'I should have left him at home, really; he's in disgrace. He totally ruined Lily Fry's party today ... um ... I mean yesterday,' she added, checking her watch.

'Uh-oh. What happened?' Elena sat down on a neighbouring beanbag and turned up the small gas heater a notch.

'He started doing the cancan on my shoulder in front of Lily's mum,' sighed Tima. 'Like ... hey, look at meeeee! And so she tries to smash him with a rolled-up magazine and I have to karate chop her away and then she falls over and grabs at a table and drags all Lily's presents down on top of her.'

'Ah,' said Elena.

'So ... don't think I'm getting another party invite in the next three hundred years!' Tima grimaced, letting Spencer run along the wooden sill of the long, low window which they'd carefully sealed with thick clear vinyl, hoping to keep the worst of the winter cold out.

'Do you care?' asked Elena, pulling a flask of hot chocolate out of her backpack. 'You don't even like her much, do you?'

'No,' sighed Tima. 'She's such a princess.'

Elena raised her eyebrows. 'And you're not?'

'Oh come on!' Tima looked wounded. 'OK—I sing and dance and stuff but I'm not like Lily. I mean ... *Hello*! One of my best friends is a *spider*.'

'Don't let Lucky see him,' came a new voice, and the scruffy head of Matteus Wheeler rose through the trapdoor, accompanied by a small, dark bird.

'Don't eat Spencer!' warned Tima, quickly. 'Lucky!' She pointed to the spider as it crouched, motionless, on the sill. 'He's not your dinner, he's my friend.'

'Friend,' echoed Lucky before settling, with a shake of her rainbow black feathers, on Matt's shoulder. A spider was natural food for a starling, but Elena was sure the bird wouldn't eat Spencer. Not when Tima had asked it not to.

'Did you see that green flash in the sky?' asked Matt, as he held out his hands to the gas fire; a small camping-sized thing with a butane canister attached. The fire kicked out a pretty good heat and threw a golden light across the room. Over the past few weeks they'd stocked the hide with rugs, beanbags, a red-painted trunk filled with their snack supplies, and the gas heater. Matt had brought the gas heater and the canister. He'd been very particular about ventilation, making sure the roof had a hole to act as a chimney. Right above the hole was a cluster of branches which largely held out the rain—and the open hatch into the hide provided enough updraft to keep them all safe from any leaking fumes.

'Yeah,' said Tima. 'Someone loves their green fireworks. They've been letting them off all week.'

'No bang though,' said Elena.

There was silence for a few moments. Weird things happened in Thornleigh and it was tempting, thought Elena, to believe that everything out of the ordinary was something sinister. Even when it wasn't.

'Some people just like the pretty ones which don't make any noise,' said Tima.

'Do you ever wonder where the beam connects?' Elena said, thinking about another kind of sparkling light. 'I mean, we know it connects with something around here somewhere . . . in a cave or something . . . but we've never really looked for it.'

'I have,' said Matt, unexpectedly.

'What? Without *us*?' Tima huffed.

'Yeah. I am allowed to do things on my own, you know,' said Matt. 'One night when you two couldn't get out I went all around the quarry cliff and the hill with Lucky and tried to find a cave. Couldn't find anything.'

'You didn't go in the one behind the warehouse, did you?' asked Elena.

Matt rolled his eyes. 'No. I'm not an idiot.'

'Good,' said Elena. 'We don't want to wake up anything in there again.'

'We need to insulate this place,' Matt said, abruptly changing the subject. 'It's going to get a lot colder.'

'It's no good bringing curtains and stuff,' said Elena. 'They'll just get damp. The rugs are already feeling damp. When we're away and the fire is out, the damp gets in.'

'Maybe we should get some foil blankets,' said Tima, pouring Matt a mug of hot chocolate from the flask and handing it to him. 'You know—like they wrap cold people in. Hang them up around the walls. They reflect the heat.'

Matt nodded and rubbed his nose thoughtfully. Then winced.

'How is it?' asked Elena.

'Fine,' said Matt. 'Not as bad as it was. Anyway, you should see the other guy . . .'

'Not funny,' said Elena. 'He's still in hospital, you know.'

'What?' Tima was all agog. 'What happened? Don't tell me you knocked someone out, Matt! You total crim!'

Matt rolled his eyes. 'No. Liam Bassiter nearly knocked *me* out. He head-butted my nose in the gym.'

'And then, a few minutes later, he collapsed,' said Elena. 'They took him away in an ambulance.'

'What's wrong with him?' asked Tima.

'Well, let's see now . . . he's a brain-dead loser . . . ?' suggested Matt.

'Nobody knows anything yet,' Elena cut in. 'He just dropped to the floor, unconscious, and nobody could wake him up. It was . . . you know . . . serious. None of the teachers would talk about it. So, it looks like it really is serious.'

'You don't think . . .' Tima began, eyeing Matt warily. 'Well, you know when you got the buzzards and red kites onto him . . . ?'

Matt glared at her. 'What?'

Tima shrugged. 'I'm just saying. I mean, I don't blame you. Liam *was* about to drop you off a fifteen storey balcony, so . . .'

'Yeah. So?' Matt bristled and Lucky shuddered her wings, picking it up.

'So . . . he was knocked out, wasn't he? Out cold. So maybe there was some damage to his brain.'

'Liam Bassiter,' hissed Matt, 'doesn't have enough brain to damage.'

'It's fine, Matt,' Elena cut in, sending Tima a warning glance. 'It's nothing to do with that. We know you did what you had to do. And look, we're all Night Speakers and—'

'If you start doing the Spider-Man speech again, I'm going to tip this over you!' warned Matt, holding up his mug. 'I *know* it's a big responsibility. I spend nearly every waking hour telling the birds NOT to attack Liam Bassiter. They really want to. But I stop them. Even though he deserves everything that's coming to him.'

Matt shook his head. 'He always bounces back. He'll be spinning out his little swooning session to get some days off school. That's what this is about. He's fine.'

CHAPTER 6

'We have grave news,' said Mr Rosen and a hush fell over the Monday morning assembly. The head teacher stared down at the wooden lectern he was leaning on, fiddling with a piece of paper. It was unnerving. He was normally a lively, communicative man, full of confidence, but Matt saw him gulp twice before he lifted his chin and swept his dark eyes across them all.

A small ping of dread went off in the pit of Matt's belly.

'You'll all know that Liam Bassiter was taken to hospital on Friday after collapsing in the gym,' said Mr Rosen. 'He was admitted to the children's ward and kept under observation while doctors tried to find out what was wrong. It appears Liam had a heart problem which had gone undetected for many years. It happens sometimes.' He cleared his throat. Over by the far edge of the school stage, two of the female teachers were clutching tissues and looking studiedly at their feet. Matt dropped his eyes to the back of Ahmed's school blazer, just in front of him. There was a white mark on it. Probably bird poo. Ahmed had been pooed on a lot this term.

'In the early hours of this morning,' went on Mr Rosen, 'Liam suffered a heart attack. Sadly, the doctors were unable to revive him. He died shortly afterwards.'

The silence that filled the room was so thick it seemed to clog in Matt's ears. Three rows ahead he saw Elena glance back at him, her eyes wide with shock. Just in front, Ahmed's dark head drooped.

'I know this will be a huge shock for everyone,' went on Mr Rosen. 'If you feel you need to talk to someone, there will be school counsellors available in the common room at break, at lunchtime and after school. We will keep you informed about the details of Liam's funeral, in case any of you would like to attend.'

Matt shuffled out with everyone else, in a daze. Elena caught up with him in the corridor and tugged at his sleeve. 'Matt. Are you OK?'

He shrugged. 'Yeah. Of course I am.'

'You don't look it,' she said, leading him out of the stream of students to a corner by the lockers.

'Look—I don't feel anything.' he snapped. 'Liam was just a pain in the—'

'I know,' said Elena. 'I know. He made your life a misery.'

'He *didn't*. He wasn't anything *like* that important. He was like a . . . a . . . pimple on my backside. That's all. And I can't pretend to be sad he's gone. Can you?'

Elena looked at him for a few moments. Then she took a breath and murmured: 'It's just a shock, that's all.'

'Yeah, well, we've had bigger shocks,' muttered Matt.

'True,' she said. She patted his arm and turned away. He felt bad as she disappeared back into the stream of students. She'd been concerned about him and he'd batted her concern away. Why? The trouble with Elena was that she'd begun to know him far too well.

How could he care about Liam dying? Liam had tried to kill him. Literally. If he'd had to pick out a student to drop dead, it would be Liam, no question. He couldn't think of anyone else he'd choose.

So why did he feel sick?

CHAPTER 7

Violent retching noises filled the air. Alistair was chucking up his evening meal. He'd been given a grey cardboard hat to hurl into but he'd still managed to spatter the floor between their two beds.

'I do wish you'd work on your aim,' Spin muttered.

Alistair lifted a dripping face out of the cardboard hat and glared at him. 'I can't . . . help it,' he gurgled.

Spin sighed. 'No, I don't suppose you can.'

'It's the painkillers,' went on Alistair. 'They're strong. They upset my stomach.'

'They upset everyone's stomach,' said Spin, eyeing the plate of macaroni cheese beside his bed. 'Once *you* get going.' The hospital food wasn't great in the first place but an accompaniment of violent retching and a drifting essence of vomit really didn't help the appetite.

Spin knew he should eat. He needed to build up his strength
so he could get home. The red blood cell exchange had finally
finished and the painful femoral lines had been taken out—with
a final vicious twinge—two hours ago. A thick dressing was
stretched across the puncture and taped firmly in place. The
wound beneath it still throbbed.

His stay in hospital had been extended by his blood pressure
issues, but in theory he should be able to stroll around in broad
daylight tomorrow, as soon as he'd got enough energy back. He
couldn't quite believe it. For a start he was as weak as a kitten
with flu and couldn't imagine walking anywhere. And anyway,
it was so long since he'd been out in the day he couldn't really
grasp that such a thing was possible. Astrid insisted it was but
maybe that was just wishful thinking.

Still, it would be good to get out of here. Two kids had died
since he'd arrived. And the second one had looked unnervingly
familiar as he was wheeled past into a side ward on Friday. If
Spin wasn't mistaken, the boy with the buzz cut was someone
from Elena's school. Liam, his name was. He was the kid who'd
beaten up Car-Wash Boy a few weeks back. Spin hadn't seen
or heard anything else about the boy until the early hours of
Monday, when fast footsteps and muted, anxious conversation
had roused him from a light doze. He'd slipped out of bed and
woozily ambled out into the dimly-lit corridor. In a side ward
a little way down on the left, the curtains were drawn around
the bed. Behind them urgent instructions hissed back and forth.
Monitors beeped and whined. A nurse muttered: 'Come on,

Liam, come on . . .' And then . . . a long silence; long enough for him to get the picture even before a man's voice spoke quietly: 'OK. 2.44 a.m., everybody. Thank you. You all did your best.'

He'd slunk back to bed, exhausted, and fallen asleep with improper ease.

Waking up this morning, he'd reflected that it was a shame he'd never got to speak to Liam. They could have been friends. Spin had also beaten up Car-Wash Boy. Beating up Car-Wash Boy was something he and the late Liam could have bonded over, if there'd only been time.

'I've got to get off this ward,' said Alistair, putting his hat of sick aside and sinking back down on to his pillow. 'It's like the angel of death is in here.'

'I don't think you're going to die of a gammy leg,' said Spin, easing himself up on one elbow and examining his macaroni cheese. Perhaps he could poke some dinner down now that Alistair had stopped ejecting his. He'd promised Astrid he'd try.

'Well, Kacey—that girl who died on Friday—she only came in with weakness and palpitations,' said Alistair. 'She was sitting up and talking one minute, just like us, then—bang—dead.' He gulped. 'It's not much fun around here, is it?'

Spin glanced at the various Disney characters dancing around the walls. At nearly seventeen he was horrified that he had to be here at all. Surely he should be on the adult ward? But no, technically he was still a 'child' and had to be in here with infants.

'But surely a badly-painted Elsa from *Frozen* makes *everything* fun,' he said.

43

Alistair said nothing.

'Did her parents ever come in?' Spin asked. 'I didn't see them but she was in before I got here.'

'No. No parents,' said Alistair. 'Just some social worker, I think. Nobody to cry.' He grimaced. Alistair's mum and dad had been around plenty of times, clucking over him. Spin usually pretended to be asleep while they were around. It was all unpleasantly intimate. When Astrid came he made sure she sat on the far side of his bed, against the wall, away from everyone else.

'Nobody came in for that Liam boy, either, did they?' said Spin. Visitors had to walk past the nurses' station and on down the corridor, in clear view of Spin's dark corner. He'd seen nobody heading for Liam's room.

Alistair shook his head. 'He had a nan, I think. But she couldn't come in—disabled. That's what the guy who brought him in told the nurses. That social worker came back, though—same one as came to see Kacey; she was signing his forms at the nurses' station today. Maybe they're connected—same school or care home or something. Maybe it's catching. That's what I mean. We've got to get out of here!' In the dim bedside lamplight Alistair's eyes glittered with anxiety.

'I'm going in the morning,' said Spin. 'I'll take my chances until then.'

Alistair shifted his caged leg and groaned. 'I'm stuck in here for another three days. That's if I last that long.'

'Do you think you might possibly not vomit for a few minutes?' Spin asked, sitting up and reaching for the warm plate

44

of macaroni cheese.

'Nah. I'm done. You're good,' said Alistair.

Spin had to admit he didn't dislike Alistair. The boy made a lot of noise but all things considered, he handled his extreme bad luck with stoicism. As Spin ate his dinner Alistair went on with his conspiracy theory.

'Two kids dead within three days of each other,' he said. 'And the same social worker for both of them. I think the council can't afford all these social workers, so they're slowly poisoning the kids.'

'Well, then, you're probably safe,' said Spin. The food wasn't too grim and he could feel his energy picking up just a bit. 'Unless I decide to attack you in the early hours.'

Alistair laughed unconvincingly. Good, thought Spin. He still had it.

'But I probably won't,' he went on. 'Not with all that puke-inducing painkiller flowing through your bloodstream.'

The painkillers must have kicked in soon after that because by midnight Alistair was soundly asleep. Spin, though, was fully awake. He was nocturnal, after all. His energy levels picked up further; he'd followed his dinner with a large bunch of grapes and a banana. So he was watching and listening when another patient arrived on the ward.

The usual hushed, concerned noises heralded her arrival. A skinny, pale girl of about eleven or twelve was wheeled in, looking half-dead. A heart monitor was attached to her. The paediatric consultant—Mr Castle—flicked through her notes, talking in a low voice to the nurse. 'Looks like HCM but we'll know more when the test results come in.'

'Three in a week!' murmured the nurse, smoothing the girl's long hair.

'It happens sometimes,' said the consultant. 'Random clusters—and actually it's only two in our patch. Kacey was transferred from Peterborough—norovirus on their children's ward. Anyway, with luck, young Megan here won't go the same way as the other two. Fifteen minute obs, please. I'll be checking back in around two.'

Spin needed to pee. And he was determined to avoid peeing in a bedpan this time. He was no longer attached to any monitors and he had enough energy to get up and get to the toilet. As soon as the consultant and the nurse had wandered off, he slid out of bed and walked, on shaky legs, down to the patient toilet. To get there he had to pass the nurses' station but there was nobody manning it. He wandered down the dimly-lit hall, feeling spaced out but relieved that his legs still worked. His inner thigh throbbed badly but he made it to the toilet without incident, did what he needed to do, and then carefully washed his hands. Water on his skin was usually painful but Astrid had been vehement about this. 'You have wounds,' she'd said. 'Do not let anything unclean get near them.'

The first small surprise was that the water didn't hurt. Nor did the antibacterial liquid soap. Could the cell exchange *really* work that fast? Spin glanced at himself in the mirror. His lean angular face was usually pale and shadowed and he liked it that way. Tonight, though, he'd have to admit he was very nearly over the pale and shadowed look. He'd taken it a little too far. His

46

face was like a blanched almond; his lips colourless and his blue-green eyes too big. He didn't mind the Dracula effect but drew the line at Nosferatu.

Also, he needed a haircut.

Back outside in the corridor, he stopped in his tracks. A shaft of moonlight glowed through the glass top of the stairwell doors. His heart surged. He hadn't been out for several nights and the call of the sweet dark air was strong. Wrapping his black dressing gown tightly around him, he pushed through the doors. The stairwell outer wall was all glass, revealing a vista of Thornleigh by night; lights glowing in the valley, dark hills and woods above it. He let the glow of the moon wash over his face, his skin prickling with longing. If only he could get out. He glanced around and up the dim stairwell. A sign on the wall by the next flight read STAFF ONLY. His ward was on the top floor and the stairs here led up only to the roof. Must be some kind of terrace up there; probably where the stressed out nurses and junior doctors went for a crafty cigarette. Spin climbed the stairs, slippers quiet on the polished concrete, feeling the delicious gloom wrap around him like a fur cloak. At the top of the flight was an emergency exit. The metal bar across it might trigger an alarm if he went through. But on closer inspection he could see that the door was already ajar. He pushed it open and slunk silently onto the roof.

The night air drifted across his face like a lover's caress. *At last.*

The roof terrace wasn't a pretty place. It was a wide, flat rectangle with an assortment of metal ducts, chimneys, and vents dotted around it. There were a few metal patio chairs grouped around a fire bucket next to a tall breeze-block chimney; no doubt where the smokers gathered to silt up their lungs and soothe their nerves. Nobody was there now though, luckily.

Spin went to the far side of the chimney where the silvery light was dimmer. He settled back against the breeze blocks, closed his eyes, and luxuriated in the darkness. For the first time in nearly a month, he began to feel like himself. It was a mild night and the thick robe kept him warm. He could probably sleep out here. Away from Alistair's moans and upchucks; away from Megan lying half-dead on her bed like a heroine from a painting. She reminded him of . . . what was it? That Pre-Raphaelite painting of Ophelia by Millais. He'd seen it in the Tate Gallery once with Astrid. A pale young woman lying, barely conscious, in a stream of water, her coppery hair drifting like waterweed.

Hmmm. Must be all that fresh blood giving him artistic notions. Megan was no Pre-Raphaelite heroine. She was a poorly kid in a hospital gown. Assuming she didn't die in the night, he'd discharge himself in the morning and never know what happened to her next.

'Where are you?'

Spin jerked out of his doze and instinctively froze, holding his breath.

'OK. Yes. We have another.'

It was a man's voice. Judging by the lack of response to his question, he was speaking on a mobile phone. He must be just the other side of the chimney. Spin sank down to a crouching

48

position, ignoring the stabbing pain on his inner thigh, and pulled the hood of his robe over his head.

'I know it is. We're pushing it. But we'll have a break after this. No more until the New Year.'

There was a pause as the other party, presumably, spoke. Then the man went on: 'She's perfect. Even better than the other two. Great colouring. And young . . . easier to train. Uhuh. Nobody at all. Edwina checked it out.'

Another pause, then: 'Dominic, relax. It'll be fine. You're on from midday, yes? So I'll make sure she doesn't go before I get back on at one. It'll be around two. I'll see to it. There's plenty of space for one more in the chamber.'

There was a beep and then silence. Spin heard a long exhalation; retreating footsteps; the clunk of the fire escape door.

He stayed put for several minutes, rerunning the strange conversation. What had that been about? Something about good colouring and training. Was someone buying a puppy? And why was this one better than the other two?

Spin got up and made his way back across the roof, pondering. He tried the door and was relieved to find it hadn't been pulled shut by the retreating consultant. He was fairly sure the voice belonged to Mr Castle. The conversation was nothing exceptional. Not at all. It could have any number of meanings, none of them sinister. So why had it *sounded* so sinister?

Ah, he told himself. You know sinister. Sinister is your thing. If anyone can detect sinister, it's you. As he stepped across the fire escape threshold and made his way down the concrete steps he became aware of a warmth on his inner thigh. For a moment

49

he wondered if he'd lost bladder control. Then he realized this was probably worse. He was bleeding. A lot.

The dressing on his inner thigh was hanging off and soaked through. The femoral vein was gushing merrily. He reached the foot of the stairs and then crumpled to the floor in a spreading pool of blood. *Damn*, was his last thought. *It took SO long to get all that into me.*

Then he was gone.

CHAPTER 8

SEVEN YEARS AGO

'I probably shouldn't have had you.'

Mum stood by the window. She twitched the curtain and a blade of sunlight plunged into the room. She turned to look at him, the brightness glancing off her face and her pale blonde hair.

'That's what some people say,' she went on. 'And maybe they're right; maybe it was selfish of me to have a baby when there was always a chance it might turn out . . . like . . .'

Cris gulped. Here in the safe cool dark he was fine. There was nothing at all wrong with him. Nothing. But if he just stepped outside for a few minutes . . .

'There was a good chance you *would* be fine, though,' said Mum. 'A very good chance. When I found out I was carrying you . . . I couldn't take that chance away from you. I couldn't do it. And, you know, my own condition, it's not been too bad these last few years. I manage. I was fine all through my pregnancy with you—it all just went away. I thought that was a good omen for you—even though it came back with me. And *you* were fine. I really thought you were fine.'

'Mum,' he said. 'It's OK. I don't blame you.'

She stepped away from the curtains and hugged him as the slash of sun vanished. In the dim pool of lamplight she smiled. 'You're such a good boy,' she said. 'So sweet and gentle.' She sucked in her breath and pushed him away. 'That's going to have to change. At least from the outside. Life is going to be difficult for you Cris. Mean. Unforgiving. People won't always understand you. Porphyria doesn't look like anything, you see. You might be in agony but all it will look like to other people is a bit of heat rash. They will have no clue how much pain you're in. They'll think you're just making a fuss. And if you try to explain about your blood, many of them simply won't understand.'

Cris nodded. 'Like Mr Crosby.' The memory of Mr Crosby, marching him through the agonizing heat, shouting at him to get a grip, still made him shiver. He had not been back to school since. Mum had been teaching him at home for nearly three months, while he went through all the tests and the treatments which seemed to do no good at all.

'And then, one day, guess what?' Mum said, with a bright, tight smile. 'Someone will call you a vampire.'

Cris blinked. 'A vampire? Really?' He grinned, half amused. He hadn't thought of this before.

'And they'll be half right,' went on Mum, 'Because you won't want to go out in the sunlight like they do. You'll stick to the shadows. And truth is, you will want their blood.'

Cris stared at her, appalled and fascinated. 'Will I?'

Mum sat down on the sofa and sighed. 'Our blood is . . . faulty. Other people aren't fighting off too much protoporphyrin every day. Their blood isn't thickening and blackening and rasping through their veins like liquid sandpaper. Of *course* we want their blood.'

'Should I grow some fangs?' Cris said, trying for humour. Mum didn't laugh.

'It wouldn't help,' she said. 'Centuries ago they used to try to cure themselves by drinking blood. From animals. Quite apart from the fact the stomach acids messed it all up, animal blood wouldn't do any good. It needed to be human—and it needed to be a direct transfusion, ideally from somebody young and healthy and not diseased. Actually, the whole vampire and virgin legend probably came from this; people making up stupid stories because wealthy folk cursed with the condition would pay their unmarried housemaids to donate a bit of blood from time to time. And of course back then, transfusing blood was phenomenally dangerous—just a thin pipe from vein to vein. Those healthy young housemaids must have died once in a while; got infections in the wounds or just lost too much blood in a botched procedure. The punctures in their skin would have looked like the work of fangs. And EPP sufferers back then only went out at night . . . or swathed themselves in black capes if they had to go out in the day. Cried out in pain if the daylight reached them. It's worse now, of course.'

'Worse than back then?' said Cris.

'Well, yes. Because back then they only had candlelight,' said Mum. 'Daylight was a nightmare but at least going inside would be OK. Nowadays there's no escape—it's the artificial light too. Strip lighting, fluorescent bulbs . . . in shops, in gyms, in hospitals . . . in your school. Modern lighting is nearly as bad as the sun.'

'But Mum . . . what about you?' Cris asked. 'How have you gone on, like, normal . . . ?'

Mum gave a mirthless chuckle. 'Normal? Oh, Crispin. I've never been normal. You just didn't know any different. Why do you think this house is always so shady? Why are the lamps so dim? Why do you think I let the trees in the garden grow so thickly? What about the dark film on the car windows? The gloves on in the middle of summer? Wrapping up like a mummy on the beach? The cool packs in the fridge? The times when I had to go to bed for a weekend and Aunty Sue had to look after you?'

Cris shook his head. 'I never realized.'

'Good,' said Mum, lifting her chin and giving him a real smile. 'I never wanted you to. I never wanted to spoil your childhood. And sometimes, you know, it wasn't so bad. And I can stand it. I can stand anything to be your mum. I just . . . ' her voice broke. 'I just never thought you'd have to go through it all too.'

'Tea,' said Cris. He went to the kitchen and made the hot

drinks, putting them on a tray with some biscuits. When he got back Mum was looking better.

'I've made a decision,' she said. 'For both of us.'

'OK,' said Cris, uneasy but also slightly excited. There was a steely resolve in his mother's voice.

'I could make you have light treatment,' she said. 'You'd have to go under a sunray lamp day after day to toughen up your skin. It would take forever and it might not even work. I could feed you carrots until you turn orange. I could sign you up for all the experimental stuff like blood exchanges. I could put you right out there at the cutting edge of medical science like a little hairless guinea pig.' She paused and took a sip of tea.

'But I'm not going to.'

'OK,' said Cris. 'So . . . what are you going to do?'

'I'm going to turn our lives around by 12 hours,' she said. 'We are not intended for the day. We are built for the night. So that is when we will live our lives. We will sleep from 8 a.m. to 4 p.m. every day. It will be easy in the winter months—harder in the summer. But we'll do it.'

'Really?' breathed Cris. 'We can do that? We're . . . allowed?'

'Of course we're allowed!' said Mum.

'But . . . what about school?'

'I will just carry on home schooling you,' said Mum. 'And you'll go to clubs and activities in the evenings . . . outside where the lighting isn't too bad. Your friends can still come around after school, as long as they don't mind playing

55

indoors in the light evenings.'

'What about your work?' Cris knew Mum was a data analyst for an international business. It occurred to him only now that she'd always had a basement room in their office in town.

'I'm going to have to cut down my hours, but they've agreed I can work from home,' she said. 'There won't be so much money . . . but there should be some disability allowance coming through soon.'

'I'm . . . disabled?'

She stood up then. 'Don't you ever think that,' she said, fiercely. 'You're not. I mean . . . not like that. You're fit and strong and amazing! You just have to be those things in the dark.'

'OK,' he said. 'I'll be fit. I can do training in my room.'

Then Mum smiled and her eyes actually sparkled. 'We can do better than that. I've decided to spend the inheritance we got from Grandad. We're going to extend the basement. We're going to have a fitness room down there with gym equipment and mats and lighting we can stand. And we're going to learn martial arts.'

'What—kung fu and all that?' Cris gaped at her.

'Yes. Kung fu and all that,' said Mum. 'Because if we're going to live at night, we need to be fit, and fast, and able to defend ourselves from stupid drunk people and criminals.'

'What . . . here in *Thornleigh*?' Cris stared at her.

'When you want to go off on your own one day,' said Mum, 'I will worry myself stupid about you unless I know you can look after yourself. So, yes—even here in Thornleigh. We are both going to do martial arts training until we are at black belt level. Crispin . . . life is going to be very, very different. But it could also be amazing.'

Cris ate a biscuit and thought about this. He felt a rush of excitement push up through him. He was going to be someone extraordinary. He knew it. This all sounded very much like the backstory of a Marvel hero.

'Mum,' he said. 'If we're going to change everything around the other way, could you do something for me?'

'What's that, love?'

'Can you call me the less boring end of Crispin?'

CHAPTER 9

NOW

'Spin. Spin . . . ? Can you hear me?'

Spin opened his eyes and groaned. He was back in the hospital bed and, judging by the persistent itch in his thigh, the lines were back in and he was being topped up yet again with more top-quality A positive red cells.

'How much did I lose?' he groaned.

'One unit, you idiot,' said Astrid. 'What were you doing? They found you in the stairwell!'

'I saw the moonlight,' he said.

She nodded and sighed. 'I know. It's been a long time cooped up in here. And hey—congratulations, caller! You've just won yourself at least another twenty-four hours, you bonehead! You're *incredibly* lucky they still had some extra. Red cell exchange is specialized. They don't just keep this stuff in the fridge!'

'I hope it works, after all this,' said Spin. 'Astrid—are you sure it's worth it?'

She lowered her voice. 'You're not reacting to the hospital lights are you?'

Spin glanced around, noting the brightness bouncing off the floors and walls. She was right. He felt exhausted but, apart from the femoral lines back in his thigh, not in pain. A small buzz of excitement went through him. 'Astrid . . . you're right,' he said. 'That's . . . quite something.'

'Yes it is,' said Astrid, giving his hand a squeeze. 'And look, Spin, can you call me Mum while you're in here? People will think it's weird, you calling me Astrid.'

Spin grinned and sighed: 'OK . . . Mum.' He'd started calling her Astrid years ago, once they'd got to brown belt in karate. It had seemed weird to be calling her Mum when they were attacking each other for at least an hour every day. She'd laughed at it to begin with, and then just got used to it. 'What time is it?' he asked.

'Four-thirty. You've been conked out for hours. You missed all the drama,' she sighed. 'It's terribly sad. Someone died.'

Spin got up on one elbow, fighting a wave of dizziness, and glanced around the ward. Alistair was still next to him, reading another wrestling magazine. 'Thought you were a goner,' he said, balefully, not looking up. 'Angel of death called but it wasn't for you.'

'I wasn't here. I had to nip out for an hour,' said Astrid. 'When I came back the curtains were closed.' She nodded to the end of the room where the bed was now empty and stripped. 'It seems the little girl at the end didn't make it.'

Spin felt something cold slide through his chest, as if he'd swallowed a lump of ice. 'When . . . when did she die?'

'Just after two,' grunted Alistair. 'Peacefully, in her sleep.'

CHAPTER 10

Lily lay paralysed on the grass. Her whole body was a mass of shifting, twinkling black. Ants, flies, and shiny black beetles were crawling across every inch of her, and only a quivering pink tongue was visible as she screamed for mercy.

'Insect Girl!' hissed Clara. 'Bzzzzzzzzzz.'

Tima's revenge fantasy evaporated as Lily, Clara, and Keira let out peels of giggles, just behind her in the dinner queue. 'No,' she muttered, as six or seven flies flew in determined formation towards her foe. *It was just a daydream*, she sent to her supportive squadron. *I can't let you smother Lily Fry, however much I want to.*

And, oh, she did want to. Lily and her friends had been calling her Insect Girl all week. Or Creepy-Crawly. Or Spider Sister. Or just Freak. Actually, she quite liked Spider Sister, but she knew it wasn't meant as a compliment. News of the events at Lily's birthday party had spread all around the school and grown into something quite far removed from what had actually happened.

According to the LILY FRY MORNING HERALD, Tima had gatecrashed the party, having never been invited, stormed out of the piñata game in a mood, then attacked Lily's mother in the hallway by throwing spiders at her, before knocking her onto the floor and viciously pelting her with Lily's presents. All because she was so jealous of Lily's lovely home and all her fabulous friends.

'Bzzzzzzz,' said Keira. 'Check out Insect Girl with all her spider friends.'

Tima turned around and looked directly at them. 'Look—if you're going to call me names, you could at least try to get it right. Spiders aren't insects. They're arachnids. So if this is all about the spider thing, call me Arachnigirl.'

'Are you calling us stupid?' said Lily.

'Why would I do that?' replied Tima. 'That would be like calling my plate round . . . or a fork metal. It's obvious. No need to point it out.'

'It's no wonder that you only have insects for friends,' growled Lily.

'And arachnids,' Tima interjected. 'Remember the arachnids.'

'The only things that would *want* to hang out with you are creepy-crawlies. You're such a freak.'

'If you say so,' Tima said, smiling, and turned back to collect her spaghetti bolognese.'

'I can't believe I ever invited you to my party,' Lily hissed, behind her, clearly forgetting the gatecrash story. 'I was trying to be kind. Trying to be nice. Trying to include you because nobody likes you.'

'You *are* very *trying*,' said Tima, pushing her tray of food along the metal shelf towards the cutlery. She knew she wasn't helping herself, but the only way she could deal with Lily was to refuse to take her seriously.

'My mother thinks you need help!' Lily persisted. 'Professional help.'

'On Sunday you were stabbing a donkey,' said Tima. 'So who needs help?'

She found a seat at an empty table and then groaned as Lily and her friends made a beeline for it too.

'Seriously?' she said, as they sat opposite her. 'I thought only creepy-crawlies wanted to hang out with me.'

She really, really wanted to chase Lily off with a small swarm. Most of the wasps had died off for the winter now, though, and calling in the spiders was probably not going to help her reputation. And anyway, Elena would tell her off if she used her Night Speaker's power just to get revenge on Lily.

Lily was now pointedly ignoring her and talking only to Clara and Keira. Tima focused on twisting her spaghetti onto her fork without spattering herself with sauce. She tried to filter out Lily's breathy conversation but couldn't help overhearing it.

'. . . care home kids. Mum sponsors one of them and that's why she was there.'

'I felt really sorry for her,' said Clara. 'It looked like she'd never brushed her hair.'

'I know,' said Lily. 'It's so sad. They probably only get a bath once a week. But anyway, she was rushed to hospital late on Monday night . . . and—'

'Are you talking about Megan?' Tima asked, suddenly remembering the pale girl in the hallway.

'What's it to you?' snapped Lily.

'I met her,' said Tima, glaring at her. 'She seemed nice. Is she ill?'

'She was ill,' said Lily. 'And she died.'

Tima was speechless.

'It's terribly sad,' said Lily. Her sadness didn't stop her wolfing down her lunch, though.

'What did she die of?' said Tima, getting her voice back at last.

'*I* don't know,' said Lily.

'Or care,' muttered Tima.

Lily narrowed her eyes. 'I do care. My mother was so upset. Not that I expect you to be bothered about that. *You* did quite enough to upset her at the party.'

'I didn't do anything!' hissed Tima. 'It was the spider that upset her, not me. I didn't bring one along deliberately to freak her out, you know.'

'You just don't know how to behave at other people's houses,' concluded Lily. 'I feel sorry for you.'

Tima gritted her teeth and twirled her fork vigorously until tomato sauce flicked across Lily's neat, clean pinafore dress. 'Oops. Sorry. But I just don't know how to behave.'

Lily flung down her cutlery and stood up, looking down at

herself, aghast. Then she picked up her cup of orange juice and threw it in Tima's face. Tima gasped and then took a handful of pasta and hurled it back with some force. Lily screamed and flung a forkful of mashed potato. Tima picked up her entire plate, tilting it on one palm . . .

. . . but her arm was grasped by a cool hand. Mr James stood over them, glowering. 'Both of you—to the headmaster's office NOW!'

CHAPTER 11

The earth hit the wooden lid of the coffin with a dull thud. Elena stepped back from the graveside and then Ahmed stepped forward and did the same. Elena was glad she'd come. Not because she liked a funeral—who did? —but because the number of people around the grave was so pathetically small.

Mr Rosen had let them know in Tuesday's assembly that Liam's funeral would take place at Thornleigh Parish Church on Thursday and that any of his friends were welcome to leave school at lunchtime in order to attend. The service had begun at 2 p.m. in the musty old church and there were only nine people present—including the vicar.

Mr Rosen had attended and so had Ahmed, one of Liam's friends. Liam's social worker, a hard-faced woman in her thirties with mousy hair and a black anorak, was there. So was his 'aunty', who was actually a short-term foster carer; a middle-aged lady, sniffing loudly into a hanky but not really crying. Apparently Liam had only been living with her for six months, since his nan became too ill to cope with him. His nan hadn't made it to the funeral.

The rest were the hearse driver and his two assistants who'd helped carry the coffin and lower it into the grave. It wasn't much of a send-off. Back in the damp, dim church, the vicar had rambled on about a young life cut short and said Liam would be greatly missed. It didn't look that way to Elena. And that was pretty sad.

Elena watched Ahmed throw his handful of earth and wondered how upset he was. Ahmed hadn't really hung around so much with Liam this term; not since that fight on the balcony of Liam's flat. A few weeks ago he, Tyler, and Liam had dragged Matt up there on a windswept evening. Liam had nearly dropped Matt over the railing. If Matt hadn't called in help from a few red kites and a buzzard, he might be dead—and Liam might have had his fatal heart attack in a prison hospital.

'It was nice of you to come,' she said to Ahmed, as they all walked back into the small hall behind the church, where a sparse buffet had been laid out.

Ahmed looked at her, startled. 'It was nicer of you,' he said. 'You didn't even like him.'

'Did *you*?' she asked.

Ahmed considered, running his hand through his thick dark hair. 'Not really,' he said. 'I thought he was cool for a while, you know? But that thing at the flat with Matt ... that was not cool.

I was, like, no, man. You can put the frighteners on someone but you can't, like, do GBH and murder an' that.'

Elena nodded. 'You used to be Matt's friend, didn't you?'

'Yeah,' said Ahmed with a sniff. He picked up a limp sausage roll. 'Until you showed up.'

Elena blinked. 'Me? What have I got to do with it?'

'You're like, his girlfriend . . .'

'I am *not*,' she said, shaking her head. 'I'm his friend, that's all.'

'Yeah, well, whatever,' mumbled Ahmed through a mouthful of pastry. 'He was cool with us all, before. Before he got together with you and that stupid bird an' that.'

'Look—just because he's got interested in birds and wildlife, doesn't mean he couldn't still be . . . cool. If you were really his friend, that stuff wouldn't matter, would it?'

Ahmed took another sausage roll. 'He's not my mate any more. He's in, like, the top set for English. He goes to the library.' He spat that last word out with disgust.

Elena sighed. 'Well, anyway. It was good of you to come.'

'Nah,' said Ahmed, dusting flaky pastry off his fingers. 'Got off school, didn't I?' And he walked off, heading for the door, attempting a swagger which he didn't quite pull off in school uniform.

'It was good of you to come, Ahmed,' echoed Mr Rosen, after him. He shook hands with the vicar and turned to Elena, smiling sadly. 'You too, Elena. I didn't know you were Liam's friend.'

'I wasn't,' she said. 'I just . . . felt sad for him, that's all. I tried

6 8

to get Matt to come.'

'Ah . . . Matteus Wheeler?' Mr Rosen nodded. 'And he wouldn't?'

'No. I think he feels bad. They had a . . . collision . . . in the gym, on the day Liam collapsed.'

'I heard,' said Mr Rosen, taking off his glasses and given them a wipe with a cloth. 'Some of the other boys saw it. And as far as I understand it, Liam chose to collide with Matt. Matt has nothing to feel bad about. The heart attack wasn't related to that.'

'That's what I told him,' said Elena.

'Matt's a good lad,' said Mr Rosen, replacing his glasses and falling into step with her as they stepped outside where the damp atmosphere reflected the mood. 'And he's doing well. I think you're a good influence on him, Elena.'

'Look . . . I'm just his friend, OK?' Elena said.

'I didn't suggest anything else,' said the head teacher, smiling at her warmly. 'Good friends can make a world of difference in our lives. I'd be lost without mine.'

'Me too,' said Elena. She glanced back towards the cemetery and thought she saw red fur at the base of the yew tree hedges. Velma was waiting for her. 'I'm going this way,' she said to Mr Rosen.

'Well, cheerio,' he said, as he turned towards the main gate. 'See you in school tomorrow.'

Elena skirted the graves and headed for the edge of the cemetery, warmed through, despite the chill of the afternoon, as she saw Velma's familiar snout poking out from under the dark needle-shaped leaves. She crouched down and stroked the vixen's head. 'It's good to see you,' she murmured. 'I need cheering up on a day like this.'

Velma didn't say much but there seemed to be a question floating out from her. She was wondering why Elena was here.

'A boy from school,' said Elena, glancing across at the grave, which still lay open, bordered by mats of luminous green plastic turf. 'He died. He was buried here today.'

Velma trotted across, tail out straight behind her, and stood over the grave, peering into it. Glancing uneasily around, Elena followed her. 'We should go,' she said. And she thought: *I don't really like standing here, looking down at the coffin. There's a boy in it that I knew. I didn't like him but . . . he was alive just last week.*

Velma sniffed around the edge of the grave and then lifted her finely whiskered nose towards Elena with what could only be described as a puzzled expression.

No boy, she said.

Elena didn't understand. 'No . . . not a boy, really, not any more. He's gone. He's . . . dead. Just a body.'

Velma flicked her tail and glanced around, then looked steadily back at Elena and sent the same message: *No boy*.

Elena shrugged. Maybe that's the way foxes viewed death. You *were* . . . and then you . . . weren't. Velma would have seen a lot of death in the wild and perhaps for her it was just that. Fox . . . no fox. Boy . . . no boy.

'I have to get home,' she said and stepped away from the grave with relief. It had been a very strange week; she would be glad to see the others at the hide tonight and try to get back to normal.

Velma growled. Elena stood still and looked around at her. What? She followed the vixen's eye line and thought, for one mad moment, that she saw *Spin* standing by a tall stone mausoleum which dominated the cemetery. *Right there in broad daylight, his pale hair gleaming under the hazy sun.*

Velma growled again and in the second Elena glanced at her and back again, Spin was gone. If it ever *was* Spin. Because Spin never came out in daylight, did he? It couldn't be him. It must be someone else.

But if it *was* him . . . maybe the mausoleum was his place. His hang out.

Skin prickling, Elena walked across and wandered all the way around it. It had an old iron-studded oak door. Could Spin—or whoever it was—have slipped into the building? She tried the door but it was locked. Elena blew out a breath and rolled her eyes. What was she doing? Glancing around, she realized Velma had slid away into the undergrowth, leaving her alone in a cemetery, trying the door to a mausoleum in case a vampire she knew might be inside.

Elena shook her head and went home.

CHAPTER 12

Spin lay still in the shade of an angel. Its face had been weathered away to a blank stare and there was green lichen on its wings, but it was large enough to provide some comforting shadow.

He knew he'd been stupid. He should be at home in bed, safe in his basement, recovering his energy. He'd only been discharged yesterday; it was ludicrous to be strolling around a graveyard in the day.

Astrid had forbidden him to go out for at least two days. Astrid almost never forbade him anything; she worked on the theory that she'd taught him well for the past seven years and he was now old enough to make his own decisions. And his decision had been to check out the funeral of Liam Bassiter. He was still feeling wiped out but also twitchy and restless. Scouring the local news online overnight, he'd found a notice about it in the Thornleigh Bugle, buried on page 18, detailing the time and the place.

Poor Bassiter's death didn't seem to have raised any interest in the local press, probably because there were no grieving parents to get quotes from—just a foster carer and an ailing nan who was too old to be bothered by a local reporter. Otherwise there would have been the mandatory school photo and a front page lead with the headline: HE WAS ALWAYS SO FULL OF LIFE and several paragraphs of other meaningless pap.

Spin had decided to snooze until lunchtime and then head out, while Astrid was at work in her study, to test his sun-proofed face . . . whilst paying his *respects*.

He hadn't expected to see Elena at the graveside. It shook him up a bit. He wasn't ready to tangle with a Night Speaker. Instinctively he hid. The blood cell exchange had worked. It was startling. From the moment he'd woken up on Tuesday, with Astrid at his side, his symptoms were gone—but it wasn't until now, out in the daylight for over an hour, that he could finally believe it. He was *normal*. Horrifically worn out by the procedure but still *normal*. Yet the thought of getting out in the day was . . . conflicting. He wasn't sure he wanted to opt back into the ordinary world.

After her decision to turn their lives around and become nocturnal, Astrid had surprised him a few months ago by suggesting he try one of the treatments she had shielded him from for the past few years.

A red cell exchange, or an 'RCX' as the doctors snappily

called it, wasn't a permanent fix but it could, temporarily, relieve the symptoms of porphyria. The reason Astrid had finally said he should try it was all about his future. She wanted him to think about university and she knew that getting an applicant's interview in the evening was all but impossible. Spin was doubtful about much more than that. He'd never really had himself down as a student.

'But you're bright. Incredibly bright,' she'd said. 'You should give it a chance.'

'I can do Open University, with online tutors,' he'd pointed out.

'I know,' she'd said. 'But university is as much about meeting people as about the study. Making connections.'

'And going to lectures . . . in the day?'

'We'll cross that bridge when we come to it,' she'd said. 'Let's just see if you can make a daytime interview first; tolerate strip lighting or walking across a sunny quad.'

So he'd said yes. He was interested, anyway. He'd had no idea how painful and exhausting and embarrassing the whole thing would be.

The funeral party was throwing soil into the open grave now. Spin got up from behind the angel and slid low between the headstones. He found a small mausoleum with stone columns he could hide behind and observe. Elena was standing next to a dark-haired man with spectacles and an Asian boy, also in Harcourt High uniform, who was chewing gum and staring at his shoes. Elena wiped her hair back from her face and he could see that she was calm and solemn; not grief-stricken. What was she even doing here? Once or twice she glanced in his direction and his heart rate went up, making his head light and fuzzy. This was really not a good idea.

After the pathetically small funeral party had finished chucking mud at the coffin and gone inside, he'd ambled over to the grave, careful to stay out of sight. He knelt on the nasty plastic turf and stared down at the casket. It was unadorned. Not even a nameplate. Likely made of chipboard. Budget funeral; the headstone would probably be granite-effect polystyrene.

'Well, they certainly got on with it, didn't they, Bassiter?' he said. 'No hanging around for you. Ward—morgue—path lab and chapel of rest in record time. Not very respectful is it?' Something felt wrong about the whole thing. It was . . . hasty. But if he had no family to speak of—just an elderly, infirm granny—maybe that's how it went; no delays while everyone made space in their diary for the send-off. No one to argue about the details. No flowers to order, no big family wake to cater for.

He heard noises over by the church hall and fled silently back to the shelter of the mausoleum, instinctively seeking its shade. The Asian kid was on his way out, stomping across the gravel path by the church hall. Feeling his energy topple and sway, Spin watched the boy go. A few seconds after that the dark-haired guy with the glasses came out with Elena. Spin took a deep breath as more weakness assailed him. He needed to go home. Although his logical mind knew the daylight held no danger for him today, his monkey brain was leaping about, chattering with fear.

But now Elena was saying goodbye and moving back through the graveyard. He realized she was on a mission when he caught a flash of russet fur beneath the dark green yew hedge. Aah. Her little furry friend was here to meet her. Spin gritted his teeth. That bloody fox had attacked him a few months back, on the first occasion he'd menaced little Mona Lisa. It was an annoying end to an otherwise perfect memory. Still, he'd deployed the black smoke and exited like a pro before her mangy vulpine protector had got its teeth into him again.

Damn. He ducked away behind the mausoleum and dropped back behind the angel a few seconds later. Had she seen him? Peering around the angel's pedestal, he could see her walking around the mausoleum and even tugging at the door. She looked puzzled; confused. Good. He could deny all knowledge of this later on.

When she'd gone he eased out of his hiding place and would have headed straight home . . . if it hadn't been for the other grave. Obviously very recently dug. It had a bunch of wilting carnations on its heap of earth and a small wooden marker with birth and death dates . . . the death was just this Friday. And the name was Kacey Barnet, aged eleven. A small, plastic frame was attached to the flowers. In it, Kacey smiled shyly through unruly auburn ringlets.

Spin stood still and stared. The girl who'd died in his ward on Friday. Also buried here. Swiftly.

If he came back here tomorrow, would he find Megan parked in the ground too? Was she already being whisked from morgue to path lab to chapel of rest at disrespectful speed?

Spin wasn't big on conspiracy theories but he was beginning to wonder if Alistair had a point. It was all eerily . . . efficient.

Spin saw his shadow sharpening against a weathered stone cross and felt needles of panic that logic could no longer fight. His head felt swimmy. It was time to get home. He fled into the gloom of the trees.

CHAPTER 13

'I'm grounded,' said Tima.

Matt snorted. 'Yeah. Looks like it.'

'I mean during normal hours,' said Tima. 'And I didn't dare come out last night because I was so grounded they might even have come in at 2 a.m. just to tell me again.'

Elena settled against the beanbag, her face lit by the twin glows of the lantern and the gas heater. 'I can't believe you had a food fight in your posh school.'

Tima looked abashed. 'Lily was just asking for it.'

'More Insect Girl stuff?' asked Matt. 'Seriously? What's a bit of name-calling? It's not like she and her mates took you behind the bins and kicked your ribs in.' He sometimes wondered whether he and Tima even shared the same planet. His nose was still tickly and sore as it slowly healed from last week's head-butting.

'No,' said Tima, losing a bit of her usual chirpiness. 'Actually, it wasn't that. I don't care what Lily and her friends call me. It was just the way they were talking about this poor girl at Lily's party. I met her in the entrance hall before Spencer kicked off the spider riot. Her name was Megan and she didn't look like she belonged.'

Tima paused and gulped and Elena sat up. 'In what way?' she asked.

'She wasn't wearing a Ralph Lauren frock and Gucci shoes for a start,' muttered Tima, with a wry twitch of her mouth. 'She was just in an ordinary dress. And average shoes. She was kind of pretty, though. Her hair was a lovely auburn colour. She was only there because Lily's mother is a sponsor of her care home. She was a charity case . . . and they really made sure she knew it.'

'That's horrible,' murmured Elena. 'Gave her the full pity treatment, did they?'

'Well, I didn't notice Lily talking to her at all,' went on Tima, 'but Lily's mother was SO patronizing to her. Megan wasn't well and she was being sent off in a taxi back to the home, with a party bag and a dollop of pity.' Tima paused, uncharacteristically, picking at the laces on her new jazz boots. 'She went to hospital . . . and she died,' she said, at length. 'I found out at lunchtime on Wednesday and it was a real shock. I mean—she was only my age and now she's dead. How can that be?'

Matt shivered. 'Another dead kid?'

'I know,' said Tima, glancing up at him. 'How are you feeling about Liam now?'

Matt shrugged. 'I told you before—it's no loss to me.' But he was lying. To both of them. He was more rattled than he could explain.

'Did you know Ahmed came to the funeral?' asked Elena.

Matt shrugged again. He opened a bag of tortilla chips and offered one to Lucky. The starling pecked it out of his fingers with enthusiasm.

Elena seemed to pick up his cue to leave it alone. She turned back to Tima. 'So how did this news about Megan end up in a food fight?'

Tima shook her head. 'It's just the way they were talking about it. I was on the same table and they were gossiping about how it looked like she never brushed her hair. She was dead and they were *dissing her hair*! And Lily was like, "oh dear . . . poor unwashed girl".'

Elena nodded. 'OK. Fair play to you. I would have thrown food at her too.'

'The headmaster gave us such a lecture,' muttered Tima. 'And then called our parents. Mum and Dad were *purple*. They are so ashamed of me, I've been afraid to move. But I couldn't stay home another night. Even Spencer thought I should get out and get some air.'

'It's really weird, though, isn't it?' Elena said. 'Two kids dead in one week.'

'I got some stuff to insulate this place,' Matt said, decisively changing the subject. He put Lucky up on the windowsill with the last tortilla chip to peck at and rummaged in his backpack, pulling out several folded foil insulation blankets and a large reel of gaffer tape.

Elena and Tima immediately got up, ready to help. He liked that about them. They were quite cool when they weren't endlessly talking.

They spent the next hour carefully lining the hut with the foil. It reflected the heat from the gas fire, and even their body warmth, back into the room.

'It definitely feels warmer!' said Tima. 'Although that could be just because we've been getting some exercise, putting it up. I like the look of it too.'

The room did look quite good. The foil sheeting reflected their images in a wobbly indistinct way. The light from the lantern and the gas fire gleamed back from each wall and brightened up the whole hut. 'We should get some up on the ceiling next,' Matt said.

'We'd better get back,' sighed Elena. 'One of these days, Tima, your mum or dad will find you've replaced yourself with two pillows and a doll and there'll be such a meltdown.'

Matt walked them back to their houses before heading to his place. Elena and Tima didn't need him to chaperone them—they both had the local wildlife on standby to defend them from any passing muggers . . . or pseudo vampires. But he was jangly and uneasy; had been ever since the news of Liam's death. He couldn't work out why he should waste a moment thinking about Liam. Liam had done nothing but make his life a misery. As soon as he'd arrived at Harcourt High he'd turned all Matt's friends against him and then picked on him relentlessly. And tried to drop him off the fifteenth floor balcony of his flat!

Matt had hated Liam. So why was he feeling so upset about his sudden death? Hadn't he wished the boy would drop dead, several times a day?

'Hate Liam,' said Lucky, suddenly, reminding him she was still riding on his shoulder and reading his mind in her random, birdy way.

'Not any more, Lucky,' he said, stroking her small, feathered head. 'You're not supposed to hate people after they're dead.'

'Hate. Not. Dead,' said Lucky. He knew what she meant; she was just verbally nodding along to what he said, but her words often came out in the wrong order.

'You love that bird, don't you?'

Matt jumped and Lucky took off from his shoulder in shock. Coasting to a halt beside him, on a bike, was Ahmed. Matt blinked and checked his watch. It was 5.13 a.m. He sent Lucky home to roost with a nod and a mental message and then turned to stare at Ahmed. 'A bit early for you, isn't it?'

'Early for me?' Ahmed waved at the large panniers on either side of the back wheel. 'I've got a paper round, 'aven't I? Going to pick 'em up. What's your excuse?'

'Birdwatching,' said Matt, a bit too quickly.

'It's too dark for birdwatching,' said Ahmed, eyeing him suspiciously.

'Owls,' said Matt. 'I watch owls.'

'Yeah, right. And your pet blackbird,' said Ahmed.

'She's a starling,' said Matt.

'Liam said you had this weird bird thing,' said Ahmed, getting off the bike and pushing it along as Matt walked on.

'After those birds went for us on the school field . . . when you two was fightin'. Then there was the balcony . . .'

'Yeah,' grunted Matt. 'I remember.'

'Look, man,' Ahmed stopped and stared down at the kerb. 'I wasn't into all that—you know? I tried to stop him. I told him to cool it.'

Matt nodded grudgingly. 'I know. But you still joined in when he was kicking my head in before that.'

Ahmed pressed his lips together and then pushed his bike alongside as Matt walked on. 'You just dumped us all, didn't you?' he said, suddenly. 'As soon as you got your little thing going with Elena Hickson and started hanging out in the library to keep her sweet. We weren't good enough for you any more.'

To his surprise, Matt realized that Ahmed was actually . . . *upset*. He shook his head. 'Me and Elena—we're not a . . . thing. We're just friends. Good friends. She's into wildlife too. And I'm into birds. Doesn't mean I don't want any other mates.'

'Yeah, your birds,' went on Ahmed. 'I haven't forgotten what happened up there. Liam was right. You got those massive birds to attack us.'

Matt took a breath. 'What birds? I don't remember any birds? It was just a fight. I knocked them out. And you knocked *yourself* out, trying to run through a door.'

'There were birds!' insisted Ahmed, pulling his bike across the pavement as they reached a dimly-lit newsagent's shop.

'You were concussed. You *thought* you saw birds,' said Matt, stonily. 'Liam just put the idea in your head.' It was lucky, he thought, that Liam and Tyler had been attacked from above.

The buzzards had struck them and knocked them out almost instantly, so they would have had no clear memory of seeing them. Ahmed, though, had probably seen a lot more before he'd brained himself on that door. Several red kites had been aiming for him.

'You're different,' said Ahmed, knocking on the shop door.

Matt nodded. 'Yeah. I am.'

A middle-aged man opened the door. 'Who's this, then, Ahmed?' he asked.

'Boy I know from school,' muttered Ahmed. 'Total loser.'

'Not your friend Liam, then?' asked the man, eyeing Matt warily.

'No. Liam's the one who's dead, Uncle,' said Ahmed. 'And he wasn't my friend, anyway. Not for ages. He was a psycho.'

'And what's this one doing here with you if he's not your friend?' asked Ahmed's uncle.

'I dunno. Maybe he's after a paper round. But don't bother. He'd probably dump them in a ditch.'

Matt exhaled sharply. 'I would not dump them in a ditch,' he said. 'And I don't want a paper round anyway.'

Ahmed and his uncle both turned and stared at him.

'You speak Punjabi?' said the uncle, a beam spreading across his face. 'Ahmed! Why didn't you tell me you had a friend who speaks Punjabi?'

Ahmed was gaping. 'He . . . he doesn't. He's just . . .'

Matt cursed himself. He'd been trying so hard to deflect Ahmed from the evidence of one of his Night Speaker's powers that he'd completely overlooked another one. The communication super-talent he, Elena, and Tima had got—along with the waking up and the lack of decent sleep—wasn't just with animals. It was with humans too. They could immediately understand any human language. And speak it. And barely be aware they were doing it.

'I just took a few lessons in the summer holidays,' said Matt, lamely. 'For . . . a bet.'

Ahmed continued to stare at him, stunned. Matt realized his former friend had chatted away in Punjabi many times over the years, to his family, in front of Matt—and Matt had never before understood a word.

He made conscious effort to get back into English. 'I've got to get home,' he said. 'Cars to wash. See you at school.'

Ahmed was still gaping after him as he turned the corner.

CHAPTER 14

Sky blue wasn't his favourite colour, but Spin had to admit he looked quite good in it. He'd rejected a junior doctor's outfit because he didn't think he could quite pull that off if he got asked any tricky questions. At nearly seventeen, he could pass for a student nurse, though—and if he was put on the spot he could just say he was new.

Mostly he just hoped he wouldn't get noticed while he was on his mission. That morning he'd visited a professional uniform supply shop on the outskirts of Thornleigh, taking a cab there and back because, although he was gradually accepting his new normal, he wasn't ready to risk a bus. The fluorescent strip lighting inside the shop made him tense but it didn't hurt him as he picked out the tunic and trousers. He got a lanyard and badge holder too, and a clip-on fob watch. The man on the till didn't bat an eyelid as Spin paid for his purchases by card.

The ID he required to slip into the badge holder was trickier. Happily, he had a great eye for detail. An eidetic—or photographic—memory, in fact. He could clearly picture the badges he'd seen nurses wearing on the ward. Back from his shopping trip, he'd simply downloaded a jpeg file of the hospital logo from its NHS website. With this, it had been easy enough to create the fake ID on his laptop and print it off on some shiny card. He'd called himself Stevan Tigori. For no other reason than it was an anagram of *investigator*. And that was what he was. Of course the ID wasn't going to work on any security panels—there was no chip or barcode on it to swipe with—but he was hoping he'd somehow manage without.

Arriving at the hospital, he walked confidently through the main reception and along a corridor towards the lift lobby. He was carrying a clipboard in case he needed to get his head down, apparently engrossed. He'd been planning to go straight down to the mortuary and see if he could get inside, but then he spotted a couple of young nurses turning down a side passage and realized they were heading for a staff-only area. This could be useful. Game on. Spin followed them.

The narrow passage turned a sharp corner and he found a door swinging shut in front of him. He slid his foot across and quietly halted the door before it closed. The black plastic panel next to it winked a red *ID only* entry light at him. He winked back at it and eased the door open. A staff restroom lay beyond it, with some battered sofas and a rectangle of lockers against the wall to the right. He heard the nurses—both female—talking to each other from behind two small open locker doors.

'That was one long shift,' said one of them, flinging a navy cardigan over the top of hers. 'I'm so done with D level. I'm going home and getting straight into my PJs.'

Spin's eyes rested on the cardigan. It had an ID clipped to it. A real ID.

'Are you on earlies tomorrow, too?' asked the other one, also rummaging around in her personal cupboard. Spin realized he had seconds to seize this opportunity. Any moment now they'd emerge from behind their little metal doors and see him and his chance would be lost. He stepped silently across the dingy, tiled floor and gently unclipped the ID badge from the cardigan. Then he turned and exited the room while the nurses were still deep in conversation and none the wiser.

He shoved the ID badge deep into his trouser pocket and returned to the lift lobby. The mortuary wasn't on the assorted colour-coded signposts intended for the general public, but Spin knew mortuaries were nearly always in the basement. He took the lift down to A Level. The corridor down here was much less busy and rather more dimly-lit, which immediately eased his tension. His sensible black shoes squeaked across the green vinyl floor as he checked out the signs and glanced down at his clipboard. On it was a list of names but only one of them interested him.

Last night he'd resisted going out—even though his instinct to stalk Elena along to the Night Speakers' treetop den had been intense. Instead he'd got online and found a directory of consultant pathologists at the hospital. How useful the NHS transparency drive was! He was looking for a name . . . and he found it. Dominic Lazaro, FRCPath. There was only one Dominic working in pathology at Thornleigh General. Spin had punched the air as soon as he'd spotted the name.

Of course, it might not be the same Dominic. All this could be for nothing. It could well be that his fresh new blood was messing with his brain and he was imagining this ridiculous little conspiracy. But he was also very good at remembering conversations and for some reason he kept rerunning that one-sided chat on the phone he'd overheard up on the roof a few nights back.

'She's perfect. Even better than the other two. Great colouring. And young . . . easier to train.'

And then . . .

'Dominic, relax. It'll be fine. You're on from midday, yes? So I'll make sure she doesn't go before I get back on at one. It'll be around two. I'll see to it. There's plenty of space for one more in the chamber.'

'Dominic was on duty,' Spin muttered to himself as he reached a door with a sign on it. *Mortuary.* 'Dominic Lazaro, duty pathologist, was on shift after 2 p.m. on Tuesday, I'm betting. And maybe in the early hours of Monday and possibly in the afternoon, last Friday.'

He pushed at the steel plate of the mortuary door; it didn't move. Fishing in his pocket he pulled out the stolen ID badge. Nurse Carolyn Murray had really helped him out. Hopefully she hadn't noticed it was missing yet. He wasn't sure how slick the hospital IT team was but doubted they could have blocked her badge this quickly if she *had* reported its absence. He pressed the badge to the black plastic panel to the side of the door. The panel's pinprick of red light turned green. Bingo!

Inside it was quiet. He was in a lobby with two desks, positioned opposite each other, a filing cabinet in one corner, with a printer on top of it, and some pegs along the wall with coats and jackets. PC monitors and keyboards were on the desks and an assortment of notices hung on a pinboard on the wall above them. There was nobody here. To his left a door led through to the cold store where all the bodies were kept. The glass panel in it showed a solitary figure working over a trolley. A pale leg was on display, a tag on its toe. To his right was an identical door and through the glass panel he could see the cold metal surfaces of a pathology lab. Nobody in it.

Spin glanced quickly around the room. What he wanted was simple—but how would he find it? Staff rotas would surely be on the computer. He went to the nearest PC and prodded its keyboard. The screen flickered into life . . . but it wanted a name and password. No good. Could he boldly step into the cold store room and just ask?

He was considering this when the door behind him opened and a young, dark-haired woman in a white tunic came in. 'Oh—hello,' she said, raising her eyebrows. 'Can I help you?'

Spin turned around and gave her a nervous grin. 'I don't know,' he said. 'D level sent me down to ask for a pixie gurney . . . ?'

The woman blinked. 'A what?'

Spin gulped loudly. 'Oh no.' He rubbed his hand over his

face, wincing. 'I'm such an idiot. *Pixie gurney.*'

She laughed and shook her head. 'Oh dear. First day on the ward by any chance?'

He nodded, grinning awkwardly. 'Yeah. If I was a trainee mechanic they'd have sent me for a tin of elbow grease, wouldn't they? Or a left-handed screwdriver.'

She chuckled sympathetically. 'Yep! Anything else I can get for you, new boy? A unicorn trolley, maybe?'

He gave her a roll of his blue-green eyes—always effective—and her smile deepened. 'Actually—there was one thing. Nurse ...um...I've forgotten her name already...oh no—Nurse Murray, Carolyn ...she asked about staff rotas down here for last week and this next week.'

The woman in the tunic looked puzzled. 'OK...not sure why a D level nurse would want that.'

'Um...I think...' Spin bit his lip, '...there's this pathologist she fancies. She's hoping to bump into him on shift so she wants to find out what pattern he's on.'

'Oh, they really are working you!' chuckled the woman, shaking her head. 'I can give you the rota—but if some nurse starts stalking one of my pathologists I'll be holding you responsible.' She stepped up to the desk, rattled some keys and a few seconds later two weeks of shift patterns and names spilled out of the printer. She handed the pages to him. 'Go on now—get back to your ward, Stevan, and tell them to give you some proper work to do.'

'I will—thank you! Thank you so much!' Spin did a little bow and backed out of the room. Outside he walked swiftly back to the lift lobby, not quite believing how easy that had been. The lift came quickly and flickered its nasty strip lighting at him but he was too gripped by the rota to pay attention to the low level prickling in his veins. There were six duty pathologists working in the mortuary. And Dominic Lazaro was one of them. Spin ran his fingers down the table of names and times.

FRIDAY	12 p.m to 8 p.m.	D. Lazaro
MONDAY	8 p.m. to 4 a.m.	D. Lazaro
TUESDAY	12 p.m to 8 p.m.	D. Lazaro

Spin felt the prickles wash over him and this time it wasn't just down to the lighting. Three kids had died unexpectedly— and all three were looked after by Mr Castle—and given a post mortem by Dominic Lazaro.

OK. None of this really added up to a conspiracy . . . did it? The same staff on the same shift patterns would oversee any number of deaths, wouldn't they?

It was just those words . . . *'Dominic, relax. It'll be fine. You're on from midday, yes? So I'll make sure she doesn't go before I get back on at one. It'll be around two. I'll see to it.'*

And Megan had died around two.

And then, just throw *this* weird thought in . . .

'Even better than the other two. Great colouring.'

All three of those dead kids were redheads.

CHAPTER 15

'I think I might have messed up.' Matt lay flat on his back in the grass and sighed.

'Wooooo! Did you see that one?' Tima pointed north-east. 'Sorry . . . what did you say?'

'I said—WHOA! Look at that one!' Matt waved towards the north-west as a shooting star arced across the night sky. He'd responded grumpily when Tima had first texted to suggest they all get sleeping bags and waterproof mats and lie on their backs in a field that night. **Lie in a damp field? Seriously?** he'd texted back. Now, though, he was getting into it. The Leonid meteor shower had been forecast on the weather report at teatime and Tima was fixated on watching it. Since learning that the nightly beam which woke them had an interplanetary source, she'd been more and more fascinated by what was out there.

'Messed up how?' asked Elena, zipped up warmly just next to Tima. The three of them were dead centre in a meadow, a short hike from their treehouse den. The night was clear and the stars overhead were stunning, even without a meteor shower.

'I started speaking Punjabi,' said Matt.

Elena got up on one elbow. 'Who to?'

'Who to?' echoed Tima, with a giggle. 'You sound like an owl.' As soon as she said this a glowing form coasted over them just a metre above their faces. If she wasn't mistaken, that was one of Matt's owl friends, saying hello.

Matt held up a clenched fist and the barn owl landed on it, flapping its pale wings, luminous in the starlight.

'OK,' said Elena, flicking the side of Tima's head. 'To *whom* did you speak Punjabi, Matt?'

Matt sat up and stroked the soft, domed head of the barn owl. 'Ahmed,' he said. 'I met him on my way home yesterday morning; he was going to start his paper round.'

'You talked to Ahmed?' Elena sat up too and ran her fingers along the owl's wing feathers. 'What about?'

'Stuff,' said Matt. 'He was wondering why I was strolling down the road before dawn, with Lucky on my shoulder. I told him I was out owl-watching. And then he . . . well I think he kind of tried to apologize about the stuff that happened with him and Liam and Tyler. And when we got to the shop his uncle runs, they started yapping away in Punjabi and I just joined in before I realized what was happening.'

'It's tricky, isn't it?' said Tima, giving up the star-searching and sitting up to join in with the chat and the owl-petting. 'I

94

keep speaking in Arabic around my mum and dad and I was never much good at it before. They like it but I can tell they're a bit freaked out that I can understand so much of what they say these days. I think they've said all kinds of things to each other over the years that they didn't expect me to get. Now I get it all ... sometimes I have to pretend I don't.'

Matt nodded. 'Me and Mum speak more Polish too. Not in front of Dad though. Dad hates it.'

'What did Ahmed make of it?' asked Elena.

'He was freaked out,' said Matt. 'He didn't expect me to understand a word. And I did. All of it. Even the rude stuff he was saying about me to his uncle. No—don't stroke her any more. It's not good for her feathers.' Tima and Elena obediently withdrew their hands as Matt transferred the barn owl casually onto his shoulder and went on. 'Now I have to find a way to explain how I suddenly speak his language like a native. I don't think he bought the "learning it over the summer for a bet" thing. And he was already asking me about the birds. He remembers the kites up on the balcony.'

'He knows way too much. We have to find a way of stopping this getting out,' said Elena with a sigh. 'We need to try to work out when someone's speaking in another language. If I listen properly I can hear when the language has changed—it's only when I'm not paying attention that I can accidentally start speaking to someone in their own language.'

'It's a cool thing,' said Tima. 'Why can't we just say we're language geniuses?!'

'Because it doesn't make any sense. Not when we never

were before,' said Elena. 'And it will get people interested in us. Focusing on us. And we don't want that, do we? We want to . . . blend in. When we became Night Speakers . . . when the beam came through and messed up our minds . . . it changed us a lot. We're kind of super-communicators. But nobody else is. I've researched it online and there's nobody else in the world that can speak every language—instantly. And there's certainly nobody that can speak owl, or fox, or spider. We're . . . freaks of nature!'

Tima lay down again and watched a speck of space dust burn up in the atmosphere, chalking a line across the night sky for half a second. 'I like being a freak of nature,' she said. 'I'd never have met you two if I hadn't got freaky. And we'd never have met Carra, either, would we?'

Elena and Matt lay down too, Matt sending the owl up and on its way first, and they all gazed up at the stars. 'She's out there somewhere,' said Elena. 'I can't believe we really met an alien.'

'If we hadn't met her this whole field would be full of killer plants,' muttered Matt. 'And we'd all be dead, along with the rest of humankind. But . . . how do we know for sure she really was an alien? She looked human enough. She might just have packed up and gone to . . . I dunno . . . Belgium.'

'She's up there,' said Elena, smiling. 'And she might come back one day; you never know.'

'In the meantime, how do we stop speaking other languages and attracting attention?' asked Tima. 'So we're not famous international freaks by the time she does come back.'

'I think we just have to listen more carefully,' said Elena. 'Concentrate. And, you know, if someone obviously has another language in their culture, be extra careful.' She sighed happily, because at this moment, Velma, her vixen friend, slipped across the meadow with two of her daughters and settled down next to her, snuggling up against the sleeping bag.

Velma raised her snout, sniffed the air, and then fixed Elena with an intense stare. 'What's she saying?' asked Tima.

Elena sat up again, looking puzzled. 'Um . . . she wants me . . . us . . . to go somewhere. See something.'

'Where?' asked Matt.

'What?' said Tima at the same time.

Elena was already on her feet, picking up her sleeping bag. She looked perplexed. Uneasy. 'I'm not sure I'm getting this right. Just . . . follow her, OK?'

They tightly rolled their sleeping bags and mats, shoved them into their backpacks and then set off across the meadow, following the three foxes. Velma and her daughters took them back into the woods towards the treehouse den, but didn't stop there. They led them back up over Leigh Hill and down a chalky path, under the railway arch and around the edge of the Quarry End industrial estate. Arriving at the roads, the vixen became more watchful, and so did they, keeping to the shadows and hiding behind bushes or bus shelters when an early hours motorist drove by. Eventually they arrived at Thornleigh Parish Church and the dark cemetery beyond.

'What's going on?' whispered Matt. 'Why does she want us to go in here?'

'Isn't this where Liam Bassiter was buried?' whispered back Tima, as they pushed open the tall, wrought-iron gates.

Elena nodded and followed on after the three foxes as they bounded fluidly over stone crosses and marble pedestals. 'I don't like this,' she murmured. Tima grabbed her hand and glanced back at Matt. Matt clearly didn't like it either. They shone their torches carefully to avoid stumbling over the headstones.

'Where are they taking us?' hissed Tima. 'What's going on?'

'I . . . I think . . .' Elena suddenly sucked in her breath and Tima saw a dim glow between the graves. There was a thudding and scraping sound. Tima's feet carried her forward with Elena and Matt, even though she recognized the sound. A really bad sound. In the middle of the night, in a graveyard, you really didn't want to hear digging.

'What the—?' Matt let out a curse and exhaled in shock. The dim glow came from a lantern on the ground. Next to it was an open grave and inside the grave, visible from the waist up, was a lone figure.

'Ah good,' said the figure. 'Now . . . I expect you're all wondering why I asked you to come.'

Elena dropped to her knees and gave a gasp of amazement. 'SPIN?!'

'Yes, Spin,' said Spin.

'What the hell are you doing here?' snarled Matt.

'What does it look like?' said Spin, hip-deep in the ground, one hand resting nonchalantly on the handle of a spade. 'I'm breaking into Liam Bassiter's coffin.'

CHAPTER 16

If he was honest with himself, he hadn't been at all certain they would come. And he wasn't nearly as relaxed about this as he was pretending to be. The notion to check the grave had come to him around midnight. The more he thought about what he'd found out at the hospital, the more he wondered whether Liam Bassiter really was in that grave.

What would be the point of killing off kids? None, that he could see, unless you were a seriously twisted government official trying to keep costs down in social services—because they'd all been in the system, one way or another. The clue to what might be happening lay in that comment he'd overheard on the roof, helpfully recorded in the auditory part of his eidetic memory.

'She's perfect. Even better than the other two. Great colouring. And young . . . easier to train.'

He'd thought about puppies. But the consultant hadn't been talking about puppies, he was sure. He'd been talking about children. Whoever wanted these kids wanted them young and trainable ... and had a preference for gingers.

If Spin was right, then there wouldn't be anyone in Liam Bassiter's coffin. And the more he'd thought about it, the greater the compulsion to get up and out in the night, back where he belonged, and check out that grave. He'd taken a shovel and a lantern—and a bottle of Coke from the fridge in case his energy flagged—and set out just before 1 a.m.

The grave had been covered with strips of turf but it was no problem to peel them back. The soil beneath them wasn't yet compacted down and it was easy to drive the shovel in. The problem was his low energy. If he'd been sensible he would have waited another twenty-four hours; regained a bit more strength. Time was running away too fast, though. He needed to know now. He was forced to take several breaks, and lots of swigs of Coke, waiting for his head to feel less fuzzy and his heart rate to slow. And in one of these breaks he'd found himself being watched.

A fox was sitting between the headstones. Not just any fox either. This was Elena's furry friend, he was sure of it. He could tell by the baleful way it was looking at him. Well, OK, so he had been somewhat threatening that night they'd first met, working up the vampire thing for maximum fun with Elena. He had to respect the fox for stepping up, even though all it got from him was a clout on the snout and a puff of smoke.

'What do you want?'

It flicked its ears in response and then Spin had got to

thinking. If his suspicions were correct, he could use some help—someone to talk it through with. Elena would be good—and he bet she was out with her little gang tonight. Elena and this fox understood each other well. They had some freaky telepathic link going on. 'Hey,' he said. 'Go and get Elena. Bring her back here.'

The fox stared at him. Spin pointed to the grave. 'Something's WRONG with this. I need Elena's help.'

The fox flicked its ears again and then turned and fled into the darkness. Spin shrugged and went on with the digging for another half an hour, until he could feel the wooden thud of the coffin through the earth under his boots. He was so engrossed in the task that he was taken aback when he suddenly heard someone swearing.

Looking up he realized the fox had pulled it off. The whole Night Speakers gang was here, staring down at him, up to his waist in a grave, mouths open and eyes wide—like a scene from Scooby-Doo. It was so comical he nearly laughed out loud. Instead he leant on the shovel and said: 'Ah good. Now . . . I expect you're all wondering why I asked you to come.'

They didn't react well. They all looked horrified. Of course, they didn't know what he knew.

'Relax. I'm not digging him up to suck his blood,' said Spin, hauling himself out of the grave and getting to his feet on the grass. 'I only like fresh. The post rigor mortis stuff is way below my standards. I just want to take a look inside that coffin.'

And that was when Car-Wash Boy jumped him. At any other time an adversary would be flat on his back at the first attempt. But Spin wasn't at full strength and Matt landed a hard punch to his chin before he'd had time to call on his martial arts training. Matt didn't get a second punch in, of course. He tried and was flipped and deposited on his face three seconds later. Spin rubbed his chin and worked his jaw. 'Not bad, Turtle Wax. Got any more for me?' He shouldn't have taunted—he was seriously flaky now. His energy levels were plummeting, his leg was throbbing and only raw adrenalin was keeping him going.

'Stop!' Elena was yelling, but Matt had no intention of stopping. He rummaged in the bag on his back, leapt up and launched himself at Spin again. With something in his fist. Spin blinked and realized his adversary was wielding a sharpened wooden stake.

'MATT! NO!' screamed Elena and grabbed at Matt's arm, trying to get the stake off him.

Spin laughed. It was so comical . . . and actually rather sweet that Matt had bought into his vampire thing so thoroughly that he'd gone out and got himself a wooden stake! But laughing was unhelpful because it drove the boy into a fury. Matt abandoned the stake to Elena and went for another punch instead. Spin dropped and gave Matt the benefit of his roundhouse kick and then everything went into slow motion.

Matt toppled backwards. His arms whirled impressively as he tried to stop himself falling, but to no avail. He dropped into Liam Bassiter's grave.

There was a splintering crack and then nothing but heavy breathing and a distant owl hoot. Spin picked up the lantern.

He, Tima, and Elena slowly approached the hole and peered down into it. Matt lay on his back, looking up at them, eyes wide and glittering with horror in the swinging light. The coffin lid had cracked and caved in beneath him. His eyes darted left and right but he was too scared to turn his head and look at what he was resting on.

'Wait,' said Spin. 'Don't move.' He leaned down, hand outstretched. 'Take it!'

Matt looked as if he'd rather bite it. But then Elena and Tima reached a hand down too, and between the three of them, they hauled him up. As soon as he was upright there were further cracks and his feet went through the coffin lid entirely. He let out a yelp of horror and Spin didn't blame him for that. If Liam's remains were in there, it would be a pretty unpleasant footbath.

He grabbed Matt's shoulders and swiftly extracted him from the grave, ignoring the throbbing in his leg. Matt sprawled on the ground, apparently too freaked out to try to attack Spin again. Spin knelt down and dangled the lantern over the broken coffin. All he could see in it was white material. Could be a shroud, of course, covering the body. It wasn't a body though, he was sure now. Because there was no smell. No smell at all.

Glancing over at the fox who was once again sitting between the graves, he nodded with respect. 'You knew, didn't you? You smelt it too.'

'What did she know?' Elena hissed. She sounded beyond furious. 'What the hell do you think you're doing?!'

In reply, Spin jumped into the grave, cracking the coffin

some more, and lifted a splintered bit of the cheap chipboard lid. He yanked up the white material and Elena gave a small shriek of horror. Then she muttered: 'What *is* that?'

Beneath the white material was more white. Thick white paper bags. Spin ripped one open and dug his hands deep into it. He stood up and let the handful of powder cascade between his fingers. 'Self-raising, I'd say.'

'Flour?' squeaked Tima. 'It's full of flour?!'

Spin tested it on his tongue to be sure. 'Shame,' he said. 'If it was icing sugar we could've made peppermint creams.'

He reached down, picked up the stake, and handed it back to Matt. 'You might need this another time,' he said. Matt took it, dumbfounded, not taking his eyes off the coffin of flour.

'How did you know?' he murmured.

Spin opened his mouth to explain what he'd learnt. And then closed it again. His adrenalin was spent and so was he. He literally had not the energy even to speak.

'Spin?' said Elena. 'Spiiiiiiiiiiiiiiiiiiiin.'

Spin felt warm liquid down his thigh again. The wound had re-opened.

'Spiiiiiiiiiiiiiiiiiiiin,' said Elena, in a voice like a distant foghorn.

Spin sank down on the broken coffin and passed out.

CHAPTER 17

'He's bleeding really badly!' said Elena, pressing down hard
on Spin's thigh with both hands. His black jeans were soaked
in blood. 'He must have injured himself on the broken lid
or something. We need to tie something around his leg . . . a
tourniquet. Have you got a belt?'

Matt nodded and slid the elasticated fabric belt out from the
loops of his jeans. They'd dragged Spin back up onto the grass
again before they realized how badly he was bleeding. He was
out cold and waxy pale in the light of the lantern.

'Give it here!' said Elena, snatching it off him. 'And put that
bloody stake away! What the hell did you think you were doing
with that?!'

Matt said nothing. It had seemed perfectly reasonable to
him to carry the stake; he'd had it in his bag for weeks. Part of

him knew it was ridiculous to think that Spin was an *actual* vampire, who would turn to dust if his heart got pierced by sharpened wood. But another part of him had to be willing to believe anything these days. After all, was a vampire really any more unbelievable than aliens or underworld gods? They'd met both of these since May.

Spin lay before him, arms wide—vulnerable. Matt could stake him right now if he chose to . . . but he'd never intended to *actually* stake the boy, though, no matter how much he loathed him. He'd just wanted to scare him. (Yeah. *That* had worked.) And anyway, the blood leeching out of his leg wasn't really very vampirey, was it? Vampires didn't bleed like a normal human.

Elena was pulling the belt tight around Spin's upper thigh now, like a trained first aider. Matt had to admit she was good in a crisis.

'We have to call an ambulance,' said Tima. 'He needs to get to hospital—now!' She got out her phone.

'Wait,' said Matt. 'That's traceable. There's a call box outside the church. Let's see if it's working.'

'Then what?' said Tima. 'We all hang around for the ambulance crew? We can't be seen here. We can't.'

'We'll carry him to the church steps,' said Elena. 'Lay him there and call the ambulance and tell them where to come and get him. Then we can split as soon as we see the blue lights.'

Elena and Matt carried Spin along while Tima pressed her hands to his wound, although the tourniquet seemed to have helped a lot in slowing down the bleeding. 'It's too bright up there Tima,' said Elena as they headed for the front door to the church. There were two street lamps, each on either side of the path leading up to it. Tima nodded and briefly closed her eyes, sending out a message.

At this time of year there weren't so many moths and night flies out and about to call upon, but a small cloud of them still appeared to cluster over the lamps and dim their light. 'Security camera too please,' said Tima, quietly, and Matt saw scores of spiders emerge from holes in the brickwork and crawl quickly over the lens of the camera positioned above the church door.

They lay Spin down on the steps. He didn't look good. While Tima ran to the phone box to dial 999 Elena slapped Spin's cheek a few times, trying to wake him up, but he didn't respond. She felt around his wrist for a pulse.

'Still alive then?' grunted Matt, at length.

'Just,' she said.

Tima came back, puffing. 'It was working. I called them and told them to send an ambulance to the church steps. They wanted my name and stuff but I hung up. Do you think they'll come? Do you think they might think it was a hoax?'

'No—I'm sure they'll come,' Elena reassured her. 'I think you two should go now. I'll stay here and run off at the last minute. They're much less likely to spot only one of us doing a runner.'

'No,' said Matt. 'You two go. I'll stay.'

'Seriously?' snapped Elena and he felt the sting of her tone.

'I'm not going to do anything to him,' he muttered. 'Not now.'

'Just go,' said Elena.

'What about the grave?' said Tima. 'The coffin and the bags of flour?!'

'We can't do anything about that now,' said Elena. 'We'll have to decide what to do tomorrow. Something really weird is going on and we won't be able to find out anything else from Spin until he's conscious so . . . just go! Both of you!'

Matt gritted his teeth but Tima took his arm and said: 'She's right. We should go. Come on.'

They ran back through the graveyard and into the small thicket of trees on the other side before making their way back to Tima's road. Neither of them spoke much until they were close to her place. Then Tima said: 'Whatever Spin knows, he can't tell anyone right now. But he's covered in blood and flour. And that broken grave is full of blood and flour and tomorrow morning, in broad daylight, anyone will be able to see it. They'll trace it to Spin and maybe they'll think he's done something bad . . . taken Liam's body and replaced it with flour or something.'

'Why the hell would anyone do that?' said Matt.

'I don't know,' said Tima. 'But this is messy. Really messy. I don't like it.'

'Nor do I,' said Matt looking down at his jeans and trainers, which were liberally coated in white flour. In fact, glancing back, he realized he'd left quite a trail of it. How hard would it be for police to trace the coffin break in to *him*? 'Look—go on home,' he said. 'I'm going back to tidy things up a bit.'

Tima nodded. 'OK.' Then she sighed and closed her eyes. 'I did think we were just going to have a nice time for a while, making our den and playing with our animals.'

'Yeah, well,' said Matt. 'Life isn't nice.' And he left her at her gate.

He ran back the way he'd come and nearly collided with Elena in the trees beside the cemetery. She gave a little squeak and then groaned: 'Oh—it's you! Why did you come back?'

Matt peered past her and saw blue flashing lights heading back along the road in the direction of the hospital. 'They came and took him, then? Was he OK?'

Elena shrugged, looking suddenly very tired. 'I think he's OK. I stayed next to him until I saw the ambulance turn the corner, then I legged it. He was breathing and he tried to speak at one point . . . something about puppies. I think he was delirious. Anyway . . .'

'Look, Tima said something,' said Matt. 'If we leave that grave open and the broken coffin and the flour on display . . . we might have trouble.'

Elena nodded. 'Yes, I was thinking that too. We need to let people know, of course . . . because . . . if Liam's body isn't there, where is it? But we need to know what Spin knows first.'

'We'd better fill it in,' said Matt. 'While it's still dark.'

They found their way back to the wrecked coffin. The spade was still there, along with the tipped over lantern and an empty Coke bottle. 'Come on,' said Matt. 'Let's get on with it.'

Filling in a grave was quicker than digging it. It took them ten minutes to get all the earth back in. Matt used the spade, hefting large amounts inside onto the broken coffin, while Elena scooped big handfuls in from the edges. When it was re-filled they did their best to tidy the grassy area around it and re-lay the green turf.

'It's not as neat as it was,' said Elena as they pressed down the earth and turf with their feet. 'But it's not too bad. I don't think anyone will notice.'

They hid the spade deep in some undergrowth and Elena switched off the lantern and stowed it in her backpack with the plastic bottle. Matt realized they were uncomfortably close to dawn. 'Time to go,' he said. 'Text Tima and tell her we've put the grave back as it was. We'll have to think about what we do next when we've all had some sleep.'

As he walked home there was a delicate fluttering of wings and Lucky landed on his shoulder. He was glad he'd sent her home to roost with her colony overnight. Glad she hadn't seen him threaten Spin with that stake. Elena had not met his eyes as they'd parted company; she was still angry with him. He was angry with himself too. He should be able to defend himself and his friends with his fists alone. Carrying a weapon was beneath him. He felt hot with embarrassment when he thought of it.

'What a night, Lucky,' he murmured as they reached his road. 'I'm so tired. I want to sleep for a week.'

'Week,' repeated Lucky. She probably meant 'weak' though. Because he certainly felt weak. His mind was spinning with the fight and the coffin and the missing body of Liam and bags of flour and his belt as a tourniquet on that vampire boy he detested. He looked at his watch. It was 5.20 a.m. He would creep back into the flat above Kowski Kar Klean and stumble into bed . . . and in an hour he would have to get up and wash cars for the family business, as he did six days a week. What did Spin call him tonight? Turtle Wax. Yeah. A surge of anger went through him.

He let himself in and made it to his room unnoticed. Dad would sleep on until seven and expect to find him already soaping up a vehicle when he got down twenty minutes later. An hour; that's all he could get now. He must sleep. Right away.

But all he could do was lie awake, watching the familiar shadow of Lucky roosting outside on his windowsill, wondering where the hell Liam Bassiter's body was.

CHAPTER 18

Oh no. Not again.

Spin awoke to the familiar sound of screaming. He was back on the old ward and Alistair was having his screws turned.

For a moment he thought it might be a dream but then he saw Astrid at his bedside with a face like thunder.

'What the hell did you think you were doing?' were his mother's first loving words to him.

'Um . . .' said Spin. 'I don't remember anything.'

'Don't you try pulling the old amnesia trick on me,' she snapped, eyes blazing. 'I told you to wait. I said you needed to get some rest and stop roaming the streets playing your vampire games. At least for a couple of days. It's not much to ask, is it? And you can't complain that I normally keep you home—I give you *such* freedom, Crispin. I trust you. I imagine you are an *adult*.

But apparently not.'

Spin closed his eyes again, considering slipping back into unconsciousness. His mind was whirring, trying to work out what had happened. The open coffin, the flour, Car-Wash Boy waving a stake at him . . . and somehow he'd conked out. He became aware of the drip in his wrist and the fresh bandage on his thigh. Ah. It was beginning to fall into place.

'How much blood did I lose?' he croaked.

'You're lucky,' said Astrid, sounding slightly less angry. 'Only a unit. And this is literally the *last* batch of red cells they have in the hospital for you. It's really specialized stuff, Spin! Thank god you didn't lose any more. Someone put a tourniquet round your leg. Who was that?'

'I don't know,' said Spin. That was true. He had no idea who'd done him that favour, although it was one of the Night Speakers, obviously. 'Who called the ambulance?'

'They said it sounded like a young girl,' said Astrid. Her fingers tapped on his tightly tucked sheets. 'Are you seeing someone? Is that what this is about?'

'No,' said Spin. 'I'm not seeing anyone. I was just hanging out on my own, you know? I must have overdone it and reopened the wound . . . and someone must have found me.'

'You were on the steps of a church,' said Astrid. 'Which you might find amusing. Or have you had a revelation and got religion?'

Spin snorted. 'Look . . . I was just walking, getting some night air. I overdid it. That's all.'

'Well, young man, you'd better not overdo it again,' came

another voice, full of fake chumminess. Mr Castle was at the end of the bed, clutching a clipboard. 'You're giving the blood bank nightmares.'

'Sorry, doc,' said Spin. 'I'll be good.'

'When can he come home?' asked Astrid.

'Well, he's nicely topped up again,' said the consultant, prodding the almost empty blood bag suspended next to the bed. 'I think we'll be able to discharge him this afternoon, as long as he promises to go to bed and stay there for at least twenty-four hours. And then only go as far as the sofa for two or three days. Or, who knows . . . the garden? Get a little sun?'

Spin smiled wanly as the consultant went on his way. He'd almost forgotten what all this was for.

'Right,' said Astrid, standing up. 'I'm starving. I'm going to get some lunch. You can sleep a bit longer.' Another scream shook the cubicle next to them. 'As soon as that's over,' she added, wincing.

She headed off and a short while later the cubicle curtains were opened and Alistair gave him an exhausted wave.

'Still alive then?' said Spin.

Alistair nodded. 'And I go home today . . . if I make it.'

'Angel of death claimed any others?'

'No.' Alistair closed his eyes, which were wet with tears.

'Sorry about your leg,' said Spin, somewhat surprising himself.

They both lapsed into a snooze. He knew he should be wondering about the unexpected last chapter of last night's horror story, but he just didn't have the energy. Then he felt someone prod his face. He opened his eyes, squinting instinctively against the light (they hadn't resurrected the black canopy for him). Leaning over him was Elena.

'Well, hello, Mona Lisa. Fancy meeting you here.'

She glanced around. 'I haven't got long. We need to talk!'

'Yes,' he said. 'I suppose we do. What happened last night? We were all having such fun, and then . . .'

'You keeled over in the grave and started bleeding,' she said, in hushed tones. 'We had to put Matt's belt round your thigh.'

'Nice work,' he said.

'Then we called an ambulance and ran for it when they arrived to stretcher you off.'

'Fair enough.'

'After that, me and Matt filled the grave back in and put the turf back on top of it.'

'Busy, busy bees,' said Spin.

'Look—we only did it because we need to find out what's going on. If the police get involved . . . well, they might track the grave thing back to us and . . .'

'Yes. I get it,' said Spin. 'It was a good call.'

'But where is it, Spin? What happened to the body?'

'Visiting time is over, young lady.' Elena jumped and looked around. Mr Castle and his clipboard were back.

'Oh—sorry,' she said, standing and smiling up at him with her Good Girl blue eyes. 'I couldn't get out another time; I've got a Saturday job and this is my lunch hour.'

Castle smiled back thinly. 'I see. Well, nevertheless, we have these rules in place for the good of our patients.'

'I understand,' said Elena, really turning on the big blues. 'But . . . may I have just five more minutes? And then I'll be out of here, I promise.'

Castle sighed and nodded. 'I will be checking,' he said, but with a warmer smile.

Elena sat down next to the bed as soon as the consultant had gone.

'If you want to know where Liam is . . . ask *him*,' Spin whispered.

She leaned in, fascinated. 'Him? The doctor?'

'Consultant,' corrected Spin. 'And the pathologist—Dominic Lazaro. They're both in on it. Probably others too . . . the social worker maybe.'

'In on what?' hissed Elena. 'What are you talking about?'

Spin leaned towards her on one elbow and continued in a low voice. 'I was up on the roof in the early hours of Tuesday, just having a comforting lurk in the shadows, as you do.'

'As *you* do,' she corrected, with a raised eyebrow.

Spin shrugged and went on: 'I overheard that guy—Castle, his name is—talking to someone on the phone. He was talking about this girl who came in that night; Megan Turner, her name was. She had the same condition as Liam. It's called HCM and it stands for hypertrophic cardiomyopathy. I looked it up. It means there's a thickening in the walls of the heart—and the first some people know about it is when they suddenly keel over. Kids are out playing football when they have a heart attack.'

'So that's why Liam collapsed,' murmured Elena. 'A heart problem and nobody knew.'

'That's what they *say* happened to him,' said Spin.

'Do you think . . . maybe they took his body for research or organ donation or something?' suggested Elena. 'And that's why there was nothing in the coffin?'

'No,' said Spin, taking a breath and trying to be patient. 'Do concentrate. I know you're sleep-deprived and so not the sharpest tool in the shed right now, but try to stay with me.'

Elena rolled her eyes. 'Sharp or not, I saved your life last night. If it wasn't for the tourniquet you could be dead, instead of just pretending to be undead.'

Spin sank back on his pillow, unexpectedly stung. He realized he'd lost much more than blood last night. He'd lost his legend. A whole suit of armour.

'How do you do it?' she asked, quietly. 'The smoke and the vanishing and the fangs and all that?'

Spin shook his head. 'We haven't got time for this. This isn't about me. Look . . . give me a pen and some paper.'

Elena looked baffled but she rummaged in her bag and found a pen and a scrap of paper. Resting the paper on a Raymond E. Feist novel which Astrid had brought in for him, Spin carefully wrote out the exact script of what he'd heard Castle saying on the roof and then handed it back to her. 'That's what I heard,' he said. 'Show it to your wakeful mates and see if you can check out the grave of Megan Turner. She's the one who died very conveniently on Tuesday afternoon. Her funeral was on Friday—in St Mary's Church on the other side of Thornleigh. Get over there tonight. You can also dig up Kacey Barnet—she's just a few rows down from Liam's grave. Or *not*.

Get out there tonight. Dig up some more flour. Then come and tell me where you think Liam and Megan and Kacey *really* are.'

'Come where?' asked Elena. 'Back here?'

'No,' said Spin, eyeing the far end of the ward where Castle seemed to be about to come back to them. 'I'm getting discharged this afternoon and going home . . . and I can't come out again tonight or else I might end up back here. You'll have to come to me.'

'Where?' asked Elena.

Spin hesitated. Losing his vampire legend was one thing . . . was he really going to give up his address too? He considered for a moment and then found a compromise. 'You know the canal?' She nodded. 'The bit before the railway bridge—there's a narrowboat moored there. It's called *The Nightjar*. I'll be there at 3 a.m. For half an hour. If you don't make it by half past three I'll be gone.'

'We'll be there,' said Elena, getting up and tucking the notebook and pen back into her bag as Castle walked towards them.

'Feel free to leave Turtle Wax behind for that bit,' muttered Spin.

'He did help save you, you know,' said Elena.

'Remind me to buy him dinner,' said Spin.

CHAPTER 19

When she was eight or nine, Tima used to dream of the life she would lead once she got out of pre-prep and up to the senior school. By the age of eleven she would have loads of cool friends who would hang out with her. They'd be really into fashion, and maybe start experimenting with make-up. They'd have sleepovers and talk about the pop stars they fancied. Being eleven was going to be so amazing.

OK. Being eleven *was* amazing—but she never imagined her sleepovers would be wakeovers . . . and that she'd spend them hanging out with her cool friends in cemeteries, breaking into coffins by torchlight.

'Are we really going to open it up?' she puffed as she lifted the bucket of soil up to shoulder height and tipped it onto the black plastic which Matt had brought along. Matt had thought it all through pretty well. With the plastic laid out around the grave, it would be much easier to scoop the earth back in again when they were done, without leaving too much of it in the grass. He'd also brought along a metal bucket and a garden spade. Only two of them could work down the hole at a time, once it was deep enough to stand in. They took turns for one of them to stand lookout. Elena was on that duty now.

She wasn't alone in her duty. St Mary's Church graveyard and the roads around it were also being monitored by several owls and one starling. So far, Lucky and her nocturnal mates hadn't reported anything to worry about.

'If we're not going to open it, why are we digging?' grunted Matt.

Elena crouched down. 'We have to be sure, Tee. Come on— let me take over now.'

Elena helped Tima up onto the upturned bucket and then out of the grave. Then she jumped down herself. There was a dull, boxy thud as she landed. Tima gulped. It was OK for the others—they hadn't met Megan. The last time she'd seen her, Megan had been a normal, living girl. Suppose she *was* in this grave, despite what Velma and Spin said? Tima really didn't want to see a dead body . . . especially one she'd met only last weekend when it was alive.

There was a crack as once again the flimsy coffin lid gave way. Elena gave a muted cry of anxiety and then a low mutter. 'Wow.'

'More flour?' called down Tima. 'Tell me it's flour.'

'It's flour,' called back Matt. 'OK. Fill it in again.'

'Couldn't we just leave it open for the authorities to find?' asked Tima, as Elena stood on the upturned bucket and Matt boosted her up. 'Maybe tip them off about Liam's grave too? And Kacey's. Once they've seen the flour in the first two graves they can check Kacey's can't they? So we won't have to.' Tima hugged herself, shivering. They had all decided to dig up only the one grave that night—and to choose the one far away from Liam's, just in case anyone *had* spotted the slightly messy turf and scatterings of flour back at Thornleigh Parish Church graveyard.

Matt and Elena were now filling in Megan's grave.

'We can't bring the police in yet—we need to find out what this is about first,' said Matt, breathing hard and wiping sweat off his brow with his forearm.

'Also,' said Elena, 'Spin's blood is all over Liam's coffin. They'll have his DNA . . . and the ambulance crew that picked him up last night will remember where he was and probably that there was flour on his coat . . . and before you know it, he'll be done for grave robbing.'

'Maybe he *did* rob the graves,' said Matt, shrugging. 'This could be his way of messing with us again. Maybe he got the bodies out and dumped them in the canal. Perhaps that's what he wants to show us . . . before he dumps us in there as well.'

'Seriously?! Why would he want to dig up dead bodies?' said Elena, shoving the earth across the plastic.

'Why does he run around at night pretending to be a vampire?' replied Matt. 'Don't forget he did actually bite me a few weeks ago.'

'And he loves scaring people,' added Tima. 'Remember he was chasing me in a cloud of black smoke the night we all first met. There's something not right about him, however you look at it.'

Elena stood up, dusting earth off her hands, and glared at Tima. 'Do you *really* think he's a grave robber?'

Tima shrugged. 'Well . . . no. Probably not.'

'You read what Spin wrote down—what that consultant said on the phone,' went on Elena. 'He pretty much predicted Megan's death the next afternoon—and now there's nothing in her grave but flour. If that isn't fishy, I don't know what is!'

'Again,' said Matt, 'Spin could be just messing with your mind. How can anyone remember all that in so much detail anyway?'

'He has an eidetic memory,' said Elena, as all three of them took an edge of the plastic sheeting and lifted it, tipping the earth back into the grave with a soft rattle and sigh. 'Like a photographic memory . . . but for sound as well.'

Tima and Matt exchanged worried looks. She felt a bit disloyal to Elena, but there was no doubt her best friend had a bit of a thing for Spin.

They pressed down the earth by walking across it, and then gently re-laid the turf. The grave looked pretty much the same as when they'd arrived. 'Let's get out of here,' said Tima, shivering. 'I'm really not a graveyard kind of girl.'

Elena looked at her watch. 'We've got twenty minutes to get to the canal. Spin's going to be on the boat between three and three-thirty.'

Tima sighed. 'OK. I suppose we have to talk to him about this.'

They packed up the plastic and the spades and were about to head out towards the gate when four owls and a starling swooped low over their heads.

'People!' hissed Matt. 'Get down!'

They dropped to their knees and hid among the gravestones as a party of very late night revellers rolled past, laughing and singing and occasionally belching. Tima found herself staring at one of the spooky stone angels with weathered faces, her hands in a wilted bunch of flowers. How had her life turned out like this?

'OK—they're gone. Let's go,' said Elena.

Lucky flying just above, they moved fast through the dark. Reading the signals from the animals around them they ran, walked, paused, slid into shadow, ducked behind cars and bus shelters, ran again . . . all without exchanging a word. The communication all around them buzzed and thrummed and spoke clearly of where to go and when. It seemed odd to Tima that she, Matt, and Elena couldn't actually read each other's minds, when they were so intensely connected by this network of wildlife.

The canal was very dark; its water oily black. Thornleigh Navigation was a spur off from the River Little Ouse which fed water into the town's reservoir—a man-made lake which sat halfway up the valley. Narrowboats would putter up the canal in the summer months before turning around in the reservoir and puttering back again. The reservoir was the property of the water board. While narrowboats were tolerated there, it was no tourist attraction, hemmed in by trees on three sides and a massive concrete wall on the other.

They found an elderly wooden vessel with hand-painted panels moored in the shadow of the railway viaduct. Naturally, Spin would be in the darkest part, thought Tima. In the beam of her torch the brass nameplate read *The Nightjar*.

As they approached the boat, two slanted doors opened onto the wooden deck and the dark, lean figure of Spin emerged. He motioned them aboard and sat down on a box seat, waving them to join him on similar perches.

'First things first,' he said, as soon as they were seated. 'If Turtle Wax comes at me again with a sharpened stick, I won't be responsible for how badly injured he gets.'

Matt snorted and shook his head.

'How about we agree that both of you have a truce?' said Elena. 'Matt—no staking. Spin—no biting.'

The boys stared each other down for a few seconds and then both nodded. 'And less of the Turtle Wax and Car-Wash Boy,' muttered Matt.

'If you can resist Freak and Dracula, I'm good with that,' said Spin.

'Fine,' said Elena. 'Shall we talk then? You were right, Spin. Megan's grave is full of flour too. So what the hell is going on?'

'I've been thinking about it a lot,' said Spin. 'And I keep coming back to puppies.'

'Puppies?' echoed Tima.

'Yes. Puppies. When you choose a puppy you schedule when you'll pick it up,' said Spin. 'You want to choose the colour; you plan to train it. The first time I heard Castle speaking, that's what I thought it was about. Puppies . . . and then I realized it was something else. Tima—you're theatrical . . . can you read the words out for us? As if you're a stressed paediatric consultant on the phone, on a roof in the dark.'

Elena handed the paper over to her and Tima, shaking her head, read out the words:

'*We have another . . . I know it is. We're pushing it. But we'll have a break after this. No more until the New Year . . . She's perfect. Even better than the other two. Great colouring. And young . . . easier to train. Uhuh. Nobody at all. Edwina checked it out . . . Dominic, relax. It'll be fine. You're on from midday, yes? So I'll make sure she doesn't go before I get back on at one. It'll be around two. I'll see to it. There's plenty of space for one more in the chamber.*'

'You see,' said Spin. 'He says "*I'll make sure she doesn't go before then. It'll be around two.*" I checked with Alistair, the kid with the gammy leg in the bed next to mine. I was out cold at the time but he told me—Megan Turner died around two o'clock. Just as predicted by Castle in that call. So what about this Dominic? Well, I did a bit of snooping and it turns out the duty pathologist—Dominic Lazaro—was on shift from midday and he did the autopsy on Megan. He also autopsied Liam Bassitter. And Kacey Barnet who died nine days ago. And guess what—it's the same funeral director for all three. All three of them were sudden deaths. *All three* had no living parents. *All three*—and this is where it gets really weird—had ginger hair.'

'Liam was a redhead,' said Elena, nodding.

'And Megan was too,' said Tima.

Spin turned to look at her. 'You knew Megan?'

'Yes . . . well, I only met her once, at a party last weekend. She had lovely hair,' said Tima.

There was a long pause and then Matt said: 'So . . . you think they're not dead. And they've been sold to someone? Like puppies?'

Spin nodded.

'So . . . what do we do with this?' asked Elena. 'Report it to someone?'

There was another long pause.

'We need to find out more,' said Spin, at length.

'So . . . it's *we* now, is it?' Elena tilted her head to scrutinize him.

Spin pursed his lips and stared at his feet. 'I've managed to get this far on my own and I would carry on alone if I wasn't . . . under par.'

'What were you in hospital for?' asked Tima.

'Anti-vampire treatment,' said Spin. 'Now . . . who wants to meet for sun and fun in the park?'

'You mean . . . later today . . . in daylight?' asked Elena. 'You?'

'Yes, me,' said Spin. 'I have to go now, but I will meet anyone who wants to join me at the Friends of Thornleigh General Winter Fair, in Gladwell Park . . . at 2 p.m. I will be laughing and eating candyfloss . . . or screaming and bursting into flames. Admit it. You can't possibly miss either of those spectacles.'

'I'm up for that,' said Tima. 'But . . . why?'

'Because sinister Mr Castle is opening the event and giving a little speech,' said Spin. 'Seems like a good opportunity to . . .

find something out.'

Matt said: 'OK. Can't think of a better idea right now. I'll be there.'

'Me too,' said Tima and Elena, in unison.

'Good,' said Spin, getting up and closing the boat deck doors. He got down onto the bank and walked away, calling back over his shoulder: 'Now go home . . . and think about what you've done tonight.'

CHAPTER 20

'And they're off!'

The jockey looked uncomfortable. Just seconds into the race he had lost his grip—and now he was hanging off the saddle at a 90 degree angle, his face thwacking brutally through a hedge. Then his leg came off altogether. He plummeted to the ground leaving one torn off limb still attached to the stirrup.

'Oh dear. I should never have bet on that one,' sighed Elena.

'You could have *asked* him to get a move on,' said Tima as Elena's choice, a tired looking Labrador, trotted to the finish line in fifth place. 'He would have sped up if you'd just asked, instead of blundering into the undergrowth.'

'I couldn't,' said Elena. 'He's got sore hips.' She walked over to the finishing post where assorted owners were collecting their pets. Anyone could enter their dog for the Fun Day Mutt

Race, as long as it was willing to have a small saddle strapped on and be ridden by a doll. Barney had been ridden, for about 15 seconds, by an old Action Man . . . before he lost his balance . . . and then his leg.

Tima had chosen a bouncy labradoodle with a Barbie rider, but hers had just spent the race trying to leap over the fence between each track and play with the other dogs. It came in last. Although Barbie was still gamely hanging on.

'Hello, Barney,' said Elena, kneeling down next to the panting dog after a smile and a nod from its lady owner. 'He misses Frank,' she said, without thinking.

'Sorry?' said the lady, blinking in surprise.

'Um . . . he . . . used to play with Frank, didn't he?' Elena floundered. Damn! She must learn to shut up about what dogs told her.

'His brother, yes,' gulped the lady. 'Frank died a few months ago. How did you know?'

'Barney just told me. He also says he's got hip pain and he wishes you wouldn't ask him to run so much. Oh . . . but he really loves you, even so . . .' was what Elena would have loved to say. Instead she did the sensible thing and lied.

'I think we met in the park a while back, just after Frank died,' she said, smoothing Barney's head and staring into his liquid eyes to hide her blush.

'Oh . . . yes. Sorry. I speak to lots of people in the park,' said the lady, smiling. 'I really miss Frank too. I don't know whether to get a new puppy.'

'NO!' said Elena. Barney was pleading with her to pass that

on. The last thing he needed was some juvenile yapping in his face day and night. His owner looked taken aback. 'Sorry,' said Elena. 'What I mean is ... have you thought of getting a rescue dog? A bit older maybe? A dog that really needs a good home with you and Barney ... ? Puppies can be really tough on older dogs.'

The woman pursed her lips and looked thoughtful. 'You know, that's not a bad idea.'

'Come on, Ellie,' said Tima. 'We've got to find Matt and Spin.'

Elena gave Barney a final pat. *You might want to exaggerate the stiff hips a bit so she gets the message*, she sent. *Get her to take you to the vet*. Barney whined; not at all keen on the vet. Ah well. Elena wandered off with Tima, searching the stalls and small funfair rides for the boys.

'You should be careful,' said Tima, a teasing tone in her voice. 'You're showing off your superpowers!'

'All right, all right,' sighed Elena. 'Sometimes I get caught off guard. But dogs are quite chatty, you know. I don't think you have that problem with spiders and ants.'

'True,' said Tima. 'They're not great at conversation. But they're very useful. See that ... ?'

Elena followed Tima's pointed finger and saw a small cloud of midges just above their heads. 'Can you show me where Matt is?' Tima asked. At once the midges got organized, pulling into a tight formation and flying in a long streak towards a large red and white striped marquee in the middle of the park. Tima took Elena's hand and they both ran after the midges and arrived, puffing, a minute later, by the entrance to the marquee. Matt was waiting there. 'See?' said Tima. 'Very useful. Thanks guys!' She waved her hand and the midges scattered and flew away.

'You're just in time,' said Matt. 'I think Castle is about to do a speech.'

'But where's Spin?' wondered Elena. She peered around inside the tent and then went outside to scan the park.

'Shall I send my guys again?' offered Tima.

'No need,' said Elena, feeling goosebumps rise. 'There he is.'

Spin . . . out in the day. It was a peculiar sight. He was wearing his long black coat but no cowl or hood. His pale hair gleamed in the November sunlight as he walked across the grass between the stalls. His face was hard to read. Was he in pain? She walked across to meet him.

'How is it?' she asked. 'Are you OK?'

He gave a tight smile. 'Well, I'm not on fire. That's always a bonus.'

There was another bonus when they got inside the marquee. Castle was getting up to do his speech but he wasn't alone. Spin let out a short exhalation when he saw another man, also wearing a Thornleigh General Hospital ID badge, standing next to him on the small stage.

'That's Dominic Lazaro!' Matt whispered as they stood to one side of the stage. 'The pathologist! I looked him up online and saw his photo this morning.'

'Also,' said Spin, 'his name is on his badge.'

Castle launched into his speech. It wasn't exciting—just lots of facts and figures about his department; things they'd achieved, kit they needed to raise extra money for. It was over in five minutes, to polite applause, and then everyone went back to mingling and chatting over cups of tea and biscuits.

Castle and Lazaro stood beside the stage, talking. They looked serious; anxious even. 'We need to listen in,' said Elena, sidling towards the pair. Spin, Matt, and Tima sidled too, until all four of them were within inches of the two consultants.

'I'm not sure this is going to help us much,' said Spin, holding a cup of tea he'd swiped from a table. 'They seem to be speaking Italian.'

'*Non è un problema*,' said Elena, quietly. '*Parliamo italiano*.'

She got quite a kick out of watching Spin's face. It wasn't often he looked surprised. 'You speak Italian?' he hissed.

'*Silenzio! Stiamo cercando di ascoltare*,' muttered Matt. Spin turned to look at him, narrowing his eyes in disbelief.

Tima grinned at Spin's amazement. 'It's a Night Speaker thing,' she said. 'You wouldn't understand.'

'Shhhh,' said Elena. Castle and Lazaro were having a quiet but still audible conversation just behind her. Since she'd gained the power to understand any language, Elena had been surprised at how many people jabbered away about all kinds of personal stuff in full earshot of others, just because they assumed nobody else spoke their language. And for most of the time, they were right. Not around a Night Speaker, though.

'. . . need to accelerate the whole plan,' Castle was saying. 'She says they only have access for another day. Some kind of inspection at their end. They'll need to shut down for a while. So we need to speed up the acclimatization and move them on.'

'The first one is ready but the second two still need more time,' Lazaro replied. 'We can tweak the gas mix a bit further but we run the risk of making them ill and then the buyers might pull out when they see them.'

'So . . . what's the solution?' asked Castle.

'I think we should go on as we are and make the delivery sooner,' said Lazaro. 'If they're being shut down anyway . . . once they've paid and collected it'll be too late for them to demand their money back for lung failure. The passage will be closed.'

'We need to wrap this up anyway,' said Castle. 'Three in a week was really pushing it. I told Edwina she should have waited longer. The sister and staff nurse on D Level have already been making noises about it. We can't do any more here.'

'Maybe pick it up again in Scotland next year?' suggested Lazaro.

Castle snorted. 'If these three suffocate, that may be the end of it. They won't be buying from us again. I'll see you at the chamber tonight. Look out . . . I've just spotted one of my patients.'

Elena, Matt, and Tima were standing in a circle staring at each other, wide-eyed, when Castle came across to clap a hand on Spin's shoulder. 'Crispin!' he boomed, back in English. 'I thought it was you! Out already? I hope you're not overdoing it.'

'No,' said Spin, 'I'm taking it easy and all my friends are here to look after me. I've got to get out and see how well it's worked, haven't I?'

'True,' said Castle, turning to the rest of them. 'Well now, it must be nice for you all to see your friend out in the day for a change.'

They nodded. 'Yes,' said Elena. 'Matt really wants to play football with him again.'

Matt blinked as Spin turned and said: 'Yes! It's been ages since we had a kick around, hasn't it? Let's go and get a ball.'

Spin grabbed Matt's arm and walked him out of the tent as Elena and Tima followed. As soon as they got outside, Spin motioned them to follow him to the shade of a large oak tree at the end of the park. 'All right, you multilingual freak show . . . what were they saying?'

Tima pulled out her phone. It turned out she'd had it on record throughout the conversation they'd listened into. The voices weren't crystal clear but they were audible enough for Tima to translate everything for Spin.

When she'd finished, closing the recording app down, Spin stood in silence for a few moments and then gave a dry laugh. 'You know . . . I really did wonder whether I was just a wild fantasist for a while there. But what do you know? I'm a regular Sherlock Holmes.'

'What's this passage they're talking about?' asked Elena. 'And why are they going on about gas and acclimatization and lung failure.'

'Maybe they're being sent somewhere mountainous,' suggested Tima. 'Where the air is thinner. You know—when people climb mountains like Kilimanjaro for charity, they get altitude sickness, don't they?'

'Why would anyone want to buy three kids from England and smuggle them up a mountain?' asked Matt. 'It doesn't make sense.'

'This chamber . . . it's where they're holding Liam and Megan and the other girl—Kacey,' said Elena, working through her thoughts aloud. 'They're doing something to acclimatize them all and because Kacey went there first, she's OK. She's had more time.'

'But the other two aren't done yet,' continued Tima. 'And they won't be ready in time, so . . . when they get where they're going . . . they're not necessarily going to survive. Someone's making money out of sick . . . puppies.'

'We need to find out where this chamber is,' said Matt. 'Those two are meeting there tonight. They need to be followed.'

They looked at each other. 'Are we putting them all on watch?' asked Matt.

Elena nodded. She glanced at Spin. 'We'll get the birds, insects, and mammals to watch Castle and Lazaro. We'll all have to be on standby. As soon as we get word that these two are together again tonight, we'll have to follow the directions and go there.'

'Good work, team!' said Spin. 'I'll see you around.'

And he walked away into the crowd, vanishing from sight in a matter of seconds.

'What's the deal with that?' said Matt.

'Short attention span,' said Tima.

Elena didn't say anything. Maybe she was the only one to notice that Spin had been shaking for the past ten minutes.

CHAPTER 21

Elena walked Tima back to her place. The only reason Tima had been un-grounded for the day was because Elena had called around in person and sweetly asked if she could come out. Tima knew her parents well . . . they would be too polite to refuse Elena, especially when she'd mentioned the charity fundraising part. But the deal had been that Elena would deliver their daughter back again before dark.

So Matt set off for home alone. Drowsiness was catching up with him as it often did in the late afternoon. If he was lucky, Dad would be watching sport. Sundays were usually pretty quiet. They would sometimes take contract cleaning from a car hire firm over the weekend, but there had only been two cars in today. Matt had done them by lunchtime so he could get away for the Winter Fair meet-up. The charity event was still in full swing as he headed out and he bought himself a burger from a van by the exit. Just as he was squeezing ketchup onto it from a pump dispenser on the counter, someone said: 'Nice to see your friend so much better.'

Matt turned around and saw Lazaro behind him, buying a coffee.

'Um . . . yeah,' he answered, awkwardly . . . because he didn't actually know what Spin's ailment was. And if Spin wasn't going to tell them, he wasn't going to ask.

'Did you find a football?'

'A football? Oh. No. We just wandered around a bit. He's gone home now . . . to rest.' Matt gathered his hot snack into a couple of paper napkins and nodded to the man.

'Ah well,' Lazaro said, staring at him with a fixed smile. 'Nice to meet you. Bye.'

'Yeah—you too. Bye.' Matt walked a few steps before a prickly rush of heat flooded through him and he let loose a torrent of curses under his breath. How had he been such an idiot?!

Don't look back. Don't look back! he told himself, but as he reached the park exit he couldn't help glancing over his shoulder. Lazaro was still standing by the burger van, watching him. Matt cursed himself once more . . . had he just done the same thing again? He tried to re-run the precise words he and the Italian had just uttered but they were fading fast from his memory. Had he just lapsed into a foreign language without even realizing it, just as he had with Ahmed? If that guy knew he understood Italian, he might guess his little heart-to-heart with Castle had been overheard.

Should he warn the others? Matt burned with embarrassment. He picked up his cheap new mobile (his last had been smashed a few weeks back and Dad now refused to buy him anything but the most basic device) and saw that it had run out of charge. With something like relief, he put it back in his pocket. When he'd got home and put it back on charge he would warn Elena and Tima ... just in case he *had* spoken Italian and Lazaro put two and two together and came up with ...

... actually, he was too tired even to add two and two. He really needed some sleep.

CHAPTER 22

Sometimes, if she worked really hard at it, Elena could convince herself that her life was normal. Just for a little while. As she arrived home, Mum was watching *Countryfile* on BBC1.

'Hello, lovely!' she said. 'Look! I made cake!'

On the coffee table was a plate with a Victoria sponge on it. One slice had already been cut and eaten. 'Make tea!' said Mum. 'I'll cut us both a slice.'

Elena made the tea and then settled onto the sofa with her cake. *Stop thinking about missing bodies and just eat your cake*, she told herself.

'How was the fair thing?' Mum asked.

'Good,' said Elena, mouth full.

'Go on any rides?'

'No.'

'Well, you're full of information.'

'I'm a teenager,' explained Elena.

'Fair enough,' said her mum. 'Let's watch telly then.'

Elena sank thankfully against Mum's shoulder. Since the early autumn, Mum had been a lot better. She'd been taking her medication and hadn't had a major manic episode or been too depressed. Sometimes she even talked about getting more work. She'd been a costume maker a few years ago, working freelance for various theatre companies. After Dad left and her bipolar condition got really bad, she'd let go of her work. She and Elena lived on very little these days; a combination of Dad's infrequent contributions and Mum's disability allowance.

God, the cake was lovely. The tea was comforting. The *Countryfile* presenter was burbling pleasantly about Highland Cattle and Elena was asleep in minutes.

'Elena . . .' Mum sounded a little worried. 'Sweetheart. Wake up.'

Groggily, Elena sat herself up. It was dark outside and the telly was switched off.

'I can hear something strange,' said Mum. 'Outside.'

Elena checked her watch. It was 9.15 p.m. She'd slept for hours. 'Why didn't you wake me up?' she asked.

'Shhhh—listen.' Mum perched on the arm of the sofa, her head tilted. Elena heard a scratching noise. Then a series of tiny thuds. Then a shrill bark. She got up and headed into the kitchen. With the light switched off she got clear view of several small furry faces at the window. There were at least six squirrels trying to get her attention. The light suddenly came on as Mum followed her in and hit the switch. The squirrels scarpered.

'I think it's . . . just squirrels,' Elena said. 'I'll look outside.' Out in the dark back garden she was immediately aware that Velma was waiting for her. With news.

She sat down on the edge of the wooden decking, glanced back to check Mum was still inside, and held out her hand. Velma slithered out of a shrub and touched her cool black nose to Elena's fingertips. *Have you seen them . . . Castle and Lazaro?* Elena asked through her wordless fox-link. Velma told her yes. *Are they going somewhere . . . now?* Yes, they were.

Damn. It was too early. 'I need to get Mum to bed,' she murmured, her face close to the vixen's delicate ear. 'Can you wait? Then you can show me.' Velma agreed to wait.

CHAPTER 23

All through dinner, Mum and Dad had been giving her the talk.

'We know you're getting older,' said Mum. 'We know that soon you'll be a young woman. And you're probably already going through all kinds of changes.'

True, thought Tima.

'Hormonal changes,' Mum continued. 'You're probably having days when you feel strange and confused.'

Tima nodded, trying to keep her face straight. Changes? If Mum and Dad knew exactly how changed she was, they'd be feeling pretty strange and confused themselves right now.

'The food fight, though,' said Dad. 'Not funny.'

'I didn't start it,' said Tima.

'Yes you did,' said Mum.

'Well, OK, yes, I did—but it wasn't on purpose. It was Lily

who went totally bananas.'

Mum let out a long sigh. 'Tima—we're worried about you. You often seem tired and your grades have slipped at school ... and then there's this whole sudden fixation on insects and spiders. Just a few months ago you'd have screamed the house down if there was a spider or a moth in the bathroom. Now ... you spend more time talking to creepy-crawlies than us.'

Tima tried to think of something useful to say. They were right. She couldn't really argue with anything they were pointing out. 'I ... I think I want to be an entomologist,' she muttered. Eventually. 'You know ... someone who studies the insect world. And an arachnologist.'

Dad put down his knife and fork. 'What happened to being a singer and a dancer? I thought it was all about West End musicals for you.'

'Well ... I can maybe do both,' said Tima. 'I think ... I'm too young to make my mind up right now.'

Mum and Dad looked at each other. Something was going on. Trying to work out what wasn't helped by the sudden cascade of scores of eight-legged mates down the patio doors. Thankfully it was on the garden side, but if Mum or Dad turned around and saw it right now they'd freak out. *Hang ON*, Tima sent to them. *I KNOW you want to talk to me but I can't come out yet. Just WAIT a bit longer.*

'We thought,' said Mum, with a rather syrupy smile, 'that we could all go away over the Christmas holidays.'

Tima felt her heart lurch. 'Um ... where?'

'Well, we quite fancy a trip to Edinburgh. And ... Dad

found out there's a brilliant place there which runs a musical theatre course for young performers. How does that sound?'

Tima gaped at them. It sounded AMAZING. But also AWFUL. She would be away from Elena and Matt . . . and the beam . . . and Spencer and all her spider and insect friends, for ages. 'How long does it last?' she breathed.

'It's a rolling course,' said Mum. 'But we're thinking of booking a lodge by a loch and staying for three weeks. The youth theatre people do a Christmas show and a New Year's Day show. You'd be in both. They get sellout audiences.'

'The change of scene would do you good,' said Dad.

Tima stared at her dish, awash with confusion. It did sound amazing. She would love to do some shows which didn't have Lily Fry in them, meet new kids, and have some easy-going fun. But right now she was all wrapped up with missing bodies and dodgy doctors and . . . the spiders were positively *disco dancing* now to get her attention.

'You're tired, sweetheart,' said Mum, gathering up the dessert dishes. 'Why don't you head up now and have an early night? You've got school tomorrow.'

'OK,' said Tima. 'And . . . thanks. The Edinburgh thing sounds . . . amazing.' She went up to her room gratefully. She needed to find out what the spiders were trying to tell her. It was bound to be about Castle and Lazaro and the missing dead . . . or not dead . . . kids. Safe in her room, she ran to the window and threw it open and several garden and house spiders, including Spencer, thronged the sill like excited kids, full of news. She half expected them to be holding one leg up and shouting out: 'Miss! Mi-iss!' She closed her eyes and let them run over her hands and forearms as they communicated what they knew.

Five seconds later a text arrived from Elena: **Castle and Lazaro are on the move!**

Tima texted back: **Yes—spiders jst told me. Bt 2 early to get out! Have to wait.**

Elena replied: **Me too. Haven't heard back from Matt yet but I think we might need him to drive. They're travelling by car.**

Will have to wait until after midnight, Tima texted back. **Can't risk any earlier.**

Matt was woken by Dad's snoring and a tapping sound. On TV the late football results roundup was still rolling and Mum was in the kitchen, on the phone to her sister back in Poland. He'd drifted off after dinner, too tired to watch or to exchange views with his father on the performance of various players.

The tapping sound got more urgent and he realized Lucky was outside the sitting room window, pecking the glass repeatedly. Matt got up and opened the window and she hopped onto his fist, shaking her wing feathers. He walked quickly through to his bedroom and shut the door. Switching on the lamp, he peered into Lucky's bead-like eyes. *Well?*

Castle and Lazaro were on the move. Damn! It was only half past nine. There was no way he could risk going out this early. He checked his phone and found messages from Elena and Tima. They were all getting the same information. He texted them both back: **Nothing we can do until after midnight. If we can just find out where they go, we can still track it down when they're gone. Might be safer that way anyway. Let's keep them under watch and try to get some sleep.**

Need transport, Elena texted back.

I know, he replied. **Will sort it. Will message after the beam.**

'No . . . don't go,' he said to Lucky, as she went to fly to the open window and rejoin the tracking party. 'Let the owls do their bit. You're a daytime bird. Have some sleep with me.'

Lucky seemed to understand. She settled on the bedstead just above him and roosted. Her drowsiness washed over him too. Charged up as he was about what they needed to do that night, he felt himself drift. Good. Sleep. He switched off the lamp and went with it.

CHAPTER 24

They got there with Starling Nav. Lucky sat on Matt's shoulder, as he drove a brand new Ford Focus through the dark streets towards the north end of the town, and gave instructions. If his dad ever found out he'd borrowed a client's car he couldn't imagine the beating he would get. Just thinking about Dad randomly looking out of the kitchen window, while getting an early hours glass of water, and seeing his son drive off the forecourt, made Matt's belly set like concrete.

'Left,' said Lucky.

'She is the coolest bird ever,' giggled Tima from the back seat. He'd collected Elena first and then Tima, and to begin with, as they all knew whereabouts they were heading, Tima and Elena had periodically said 'left,' or 'right' or 'straight on', but as the journey continued they became less sure of how to reach the location their friends were mentally relaying to them, and that's when Lucky had suddenly begun chiming in, in a freakily accurate copy of Elena's or Tima's voice.

Matt could probably have picked up the gist of her directions through their telepathy but it was certainly much clearer once Lucky starting talking. Animal telepathy could get fuzzy when everyone was so highly charged.

As far as they could all tell, Castle and Lazaro had travelled up into the hills at the north end of the town, to a big lake surrounded by trees. They had gone by car and were still in the area. The animals were a little vague on precisely where the two were but the lake was coming through very clearly.

'Maybe one of them has a lakeside place and that's where they're keeping the kids,' Tima suggested. 'Far away from anyone who might hear them shouting.'

'They wouldn't shout,' said Elena, 'if they were drugged. And that wouldn't be a problem for these guys, would it?'

Matt shook his head. 'I still can't believe this is really happening.'

'Right,' said Lucky, as if she agreed with him. Matt turned right onto a narrow road which wound up steeply into woodland.

'Bad people,' said Tima, 'do bad things for money.'

CHAPTER 25

FOUR YEARS AGO

'Bad people are out there.' Astrid stood by the window and took a long deep breath. 'But if I kept you cocooned in here forever with me, I might be worse.'

Spin stood by the door, his heart rate speeding. He was tall for his age and might pass for a boy in his late teens, in the dark . . . from a distance. He was only thirteen, though, and very few parents let thirteen-year-olds go wandering around on their own past midnight.

He stepped into the garden and his mother followed. He wasn't halfway to the little gate at the back before she launched the attack. From behind. With no warning. She gave it her all, too, a running kick leap out of nowhere. He flipped her over in a somersault and had her pinned to the grass a second later.

'OK,' she croaked. 'OK . . . let me up.'

Spin felt bad. There could have been knotty roots underneath her—it wasn't the same as on the mats inside. Astrid got up and wiped soil and twigs off her backside. 'I feel much better now,' she said. 'You're ready. Go out and have some fun but don't stay out too long, OK? Sun will be up in three hours.'

Spin suddenly gave her a hug. They were in physical contact a lot these days, but it was rarely affectionate. It was competitive and stinging. 'I'll be all right, Mum,' he said.

She smiled. 'I like it when you call me Mum.'

'I'll probably be bored to tears out there, anyway,' he said, pulling the hood of his zip-up top over his hair. 'But . . . as you say . . . I need to get some fresh air and I can't spend every night in the garden like a pet dog.'

'Just don't start hanging around with burglars or drug dealers or . . . security guards,' said Astrid. She obviously couldn't imagine who else would be out there. They'd had trips out together, of course. They'd been to the theatre many times, to late night nature walks with bat or owl experts, shopping at open-air markets in the winter evenings.

But hanging out only with your mum was not healthy for a young man and they both knew it. Spin's school friends had lost touch with him. He'd never had many mates to start with and most of them grew bored with his shadowy world after a handful of visits. There were other kids with porphyria, of course—he'd met them through support groups—but it was a rare condition and there was nobody around his age within a three-hour drive.

'When you're older it will be easier,' said Astrid. 'When you go off to university . . . well it's all about the nightlife for students, isn't it? Most of them don't get up until mid-afternoon.'

Spin hadn't commented. He couldn't imagine himself at university. Or anywhere with normal people. Right now, all he wanted to was to spend some time on his own. Outside. In the dark.

'Got to go,' he said. 'Drug dealers to meet.'

Astrid whacked his shoulder as he headed off down the garden. The wrought-iron gate in the high brick wall was securely locked, but he knew the combination. He spun the lock open and headed out, letting Astrid re-lock the gate behind him. He would be able to reach through and unlock it again on his return.

The night was warm, even under the trees; an August night with a bright white moon which managed to filter past the leaves in chinks and dance across the woodland floor. A ten-minute walk brought him to the canal, where he climbed aboard their narrowboat—*The Nightjar*—and sat on the deck just enjoying his solitary visit. He and Astrid had got the boat a year ago, fixed its engine, repainted it and refurbished the cabin. They'd had a few evening trips out in it.

After ten minutes he grew bored, so he jumped back

onto the canal path and followed it under the railway viaduct bridge, up over the steep embankment and down to the road that led into the eastern end of Thornleigh. It wasn't really a big deal, being out alone. Thornleigh was hardly London or Leeds or Glasgow. The crime rate was pretty low. The odds of meeting anyone on nefarious business were—CRUNCH!

The sudden impact was such a shock Spin didn't have time to react. He realized someone had jumped him from above. They must have been up on the high brick wall of the railway embankment. Spin was on the ground and sprawling like a classic victim, not knowing what had hit him.

'Phone. Money. Give it!' hissed a phlegmy voice. A man, reeking of beer and sweat, pinning him to the pavement.

'Wait . . . let me just . . . ' he heard himself gasp.

Then he flipped the guy over so *he* was on the ground. The mugger let out a grunt of shock and anger and tried to punch up at him. Spin grabbed the incoming fist in his and twisted the guy's arm sideways, eliciting a cry of pain. Then he knelt on the mugger's chest and stared down at him. His attacker was scrawny and bedraggled looking, with greasy hair and a stubbly chin.

'I just need . . . some dough,' he pleaded, wheezing under the weight of Spin's knees. 'Don't hurt me.'

'Like you weren't going to hurt me,' hissed Spin, anger flooding through him. What had he been telling himself about odds?

The man stared up at him and his face stretched into a mask of fear. Spin realized he was bathed in the light of the full moon; his pale blond hair gleaming and his translucent skin no doubt adding to the ghostly effect. On impulse he ran his fingers over the mugger's throat. 'Is your blood . . . pure?' he said in a low, gravelly voice, channelling the many Hammer Horror movies he'd seen.

The mugger shrieked. 'Don't! Don't bite me!'

Spin's canine teeth had always been quite pointed. He grinned widely and let them show. The mugger squealed again. Spin began to worry that they'd be heard so he leapt to his feet and stood back as the man struggled up, wiping panicky dribble off his chin, eyes wide with fear. Spin palmed his pen torch out of his pocket, switched it on and uplit his face in cold blue. 'You are unclean,' he whispered. 'GO!'

The man legged it, whimpering, along the pavement and under the railway arch leaving Spin standing in the shadow of the bridge, trembling. Five seconds later he was doubled up with laughter as the adrenalin shook its way through him. What *were* the odds, seriously?

'No . . . *behave* yourself,' he said. 'The BPA would take a very dim view of this.'

Over the years he and Mum had attended many meetings with the British Porphyria Association. It was a chance for sufferers to meet up and share. But few of the adults were impressed with the whole vampire legend connection—some found it deeply offensive. The younger ones thought it was quite cool but this thinking was definitely not encouraged. 'Give them a break,' Astrid had said to him. 'They've been dealing with this for a lot longer than you have. The novelty wears off. It's not funny any more.'

It was funny tonight, though. He decided to head back. Not because he was shaken up. Well, he *was* shaken up but in a good way. The drunken mugger had inspired him.

'You're back early,' said Astrid as he opened the door.

'Mum . . .' he said, because he knew she liked it. 'Do you think you could make me a cape? Black . . . red lining?'

CHAPTER 26

NOW

It was nearly 1 a.m. when he woke up. He sat up and stretched and for the first time in weeks, felt better. He must have slept a total of seventeen hours in the last twenty-four. When he'd left the Insomnia Gang at the canal in the dark of Sunday morning he'd gone straight home and back to bed and was asleep before dawn. He'd risen at midday for some lunch and then headed out to the park for their Winter Fair meet-up.

Walking through the bright sun of a winter's day had been terrifying. He hoped it hadn't been obvious. He'd been hiding from daylight for so many years his whole system was screaming at him to duck away into every dark corner he saw. Simply walking a straight path between all the stalls and tents and keeping his head up was a ferocious act of will. He had been shaking with the effort.

But the blood exchange *was* working. Physically he had felt absolutely fine—in a park at midday! The thought was more than a little mind-blowing. He would always be a night owl but . . . to have the choice to go out in the day . . . to live without fear.

Of course, some people called it The Mayfly Cure. He wasn't going to think about that right now.

When he'd got back in the late afternoon, he'd headed straight back to bed and slept for another six hours until Astrid had come in with a tray of food and drink. He'd consumed the meal hungrily and then, minutes later, had drifted off again.

And now he was feeling much more like his old self.

Spin got up with a bounce and walked across the floor of his basement room, his long, lean frame reflected in the wall-to-ceiling mirror at the gym end. He reached up to the high bar and did ten chin-ups without a problem. All good. He wandered into the shower, doused himself liberally with first very hot and then very cold water, stepped out, towelled off and then went to his wardrobe to pull out his regulation black gear.

At the back of the wardrobe, like a deceased fruit bat, hung his old cape. Astrid had made that for him when he was thirteen and had just started experimenting with the whole vampire look. She had protested on behalf of other EPP sufferers—various support groups did not approve of playing up the vampire thing—but not for long. The idea perked him up and she cared more about his fun and confidence than other people's disapproval. 'It's a goth phase,' she'd shrugged, handing the cape to him. 'You'll grow out of it.'

He'd moved down to the basement shortly after turning thirteen, making the subterranean chamber his own. It fitted the persona he was growing around himself. The cape had seemed wildly cool to him at the time; now it was laughable. He'd soon realized what a liability it was. Climbing, leaping, free running through woods, along the tops of walls and across roofs, the last thing you needed was some cape flapping around behind you like a flag. A couple of times it had caught and his sinister new look had very nearly broken his neck. He didn't mind looking like death, but he didn't actually want to *be* dead. He'd got online and found the black silk trench coat instead. Light and warm, it was perfect for his look and his acrobatic tricks. It also offered many pocket and sleeve benefits once he'd started using tricks to improve his theatrics. Astrid put in the red lining and multiple pouches for smoke bombs, light tricks, fangs, blood capsules . . .

It was time to get out and see what was happening in the—
Spin suddenly stopped in the action of pulling on his black sweatshirt, feeling like an idiot. Those Night Speaker head cases must be out now, hunting down the undead kids. Now . . . here was a problem. How was he supposed to *find* them? He didn't have the benefit of pals in every hedge and tree to whisper to him.

But . . . he *did* have Elena's mobile phone number. He could call her. Although it was the kind of thing he would never normally do. Mobile phones were not his thing. It didn't really work with the legend, did it? Someone like him . . . someone born of the dark . . . texting 'Hi Babes. Where r u? LOLZ'

No. Not that. But a call, maybe. He picked up the house

phone from its cradle and keyed in Elena's number, helpfully stored in the memory banks of his brain. It rang three times and then went to voicemail.

Spin continued getting dressed, pulled on his boots, shrugged into his black coat (the warmer version for winter months which Astrid had also adapted for him with super-lightweight fleece beneath the red lining), checked he had all his usual kit in the pockets and sleeves, and went out into the night.

Out in the woods he stopped, realizing, for perhaps the first time in four years, that he really had no clue where to go or what to do.

CHAPTER 27

A black BMW was the only other vehicle in the gravel car park as Matt drove the Ford in past the gates. As soon as he killed the headlights darkness flooded them. But within a few seconds their eyes had adjusted and they could all see the soft glow of distant street lights against the cloudy night sky to the south. They could also see the gleam of the water.

Thornleigh reservoir and the woodland surrounding it was open to walkers but there wasn't much else here. Camping wasn't permitted—nor was fishing.

'Is that their car?' said Tima.

'Yes,' said Matt.

'OK. Let's get out and track them,' she said.

They got out of the Ford and closed the doors quietly.

'My guys aren't easy to see,' said Tima. 'I can sense them but it might be easier if we follow Lucky.'

'Or that guy,' said Elena and they all stopped and stared.

A few metres away a stag had silently emerged from the trees and now stood in the centre of the path, gazing at Elena. 'Oh . . . you beauty,' she murmured and walked towards it. The stag lifted its snout towards her, catching her scent, and stood quite still as she held out her hand. In the chill night air, its breath rose in a cloud as it snuffled against her fingers. Matt and Tima held themselves back, as the stag dipped its head and Elena leaned in, nose to nose with the magnificent creature. She shivered at the privilege and inhaled the warm, grassy scent of the stag's breath.

'OK,' she said, eventually. 'He's going to lead us there. It's about ten minutes' walk. We need to stay quiet and keep the torchlight low.'

They followed the stag along the path, Lucky silently riding Matt's left shoulder, and diverted through some trees and bushes. Elena realized the stag had come because it was best suited to taking them along paths they could get through. Smaller creatures might have enthusiastically dragged them through thick undergrowth until they were stuck—but if a stag could get through, so could they.

It eventually brought them to a thicket of holly trees and tangled brambles which sprawled down to the western end of the reservoir and drew to a halt. The water lapped quietly against the steep bank. There was no sign of Castle and Lazaro. 'Is this as far as you can take us?' asked Elena. The stag motioned its antlers to the left and then bounded back into the woods.

They stood, peering around, keeping their torches trained on their feet and any flashes of light to a minimum, in case anyone was watching them from a distance.

'What now?' whispered Tima.

Elena walked carefully amid the trailing brambles, in the direction the stag had indicated. She shone her torch into the undergrowth and then gave a low exclamation. 'Look . . . it's some kind of building.'

Matt and Tima caught up with her, adding their torchlight, and a red-brick structure emerged from the dark. Swamped by brambles and weeds though it was, a clear path had been made through to it. The brambles and nettles were stamped down. The path led around the corner of the structure which wasn't much bigger than a small garden shed. Rounding the corner, Elena saw an old wooden door set into the brick. She stopped, listening hard, and Tima and Matt did the same.

'Woodlice say it's open,' hissed Tima, eventually. 'Push!'

Elena gave the door a prod and it swung inward, revealing a faint glow. Ahead of them lay a set of concrete steps, leading down into a dimly lit space. They glanced at each other and went in. The light which filtered up the steps seemed to be constantly moving as they descended. Below them was a concrete platform with a metal railing along it, and half a metre below that was the water, slopping gently against the structure. On either side of the platform were two industrial lozenge-shaped lights, fixed to the brick walls and shining out dimly through years of grime. Attached to the concrete platform, to the left of the walkway, was a flat metal stick, reaching down into the water alongside a set of steep metal steps.

'It's a monitoring station,' murmured Matt. 'We did this in school. They measure how high the water is with that.' He pointed to the flat metal stick, which was marked in feet and inches on one side and metres and centimetres on the other.

'Yeah,' whispered Elena. 'But what is *that*?'

They went to the guard rail and peered down into the water. The weird movement of the light wasn't down to a reflection of the moon; it was a cloudy night. The light was actually *in* the water. There was some kind of shaft down there, sending up a blueish glow. Matt went to the metal steps and climbed down them, soaking his feet as the lake swallowed them on the lower steps. Lucky fluttered her wings and clung tightly to his jacket. She was not a water bird.

'It's some kind of . . . underwater chamber,' he called up, his muted voice slapping back against the walls and ceilings. 'Like a diving bell! There's a hatch on the top, with a wheel, like you get on the doors in a submarine.'

Elena and Tima followed him down the steps. 'Is this it?' breathed Elena. 'Is this the chamber they were talking about?'

'Looks like it,' said Matt, trying to see through the ever-shifting refraction of the water. It was hard to work out how far below the surface the access point was, but it looked like only a metre or so, judging by the helpful ruler on the wall.

'But . . . how would you get into it?' asked Tima. 'If you got down there and tried to open it up it would just flood, wouldn't it?'

Matt suddenly swung out, one hand anchoring him to the

metal steps, ducking his head down and making Lucky give up and fly to a safer roost on the guard rail. He shone his torch underneath the platform. 'Look,' he said. They stooped and peered after his torch. Set into a niche in the underside of the concrete was a large, oval red button. Elena couldn't see any wiring attached to it or chased into the concrete. It just sat there, waiting to be pressed.

They stood up and looked at each other. Matt and Tima's faces were momentarily painted green as another one of those silent fireworks went off somewhere above Thornleigh. 'Should we?' asked Elena.

'Well, duh!' said Matt and before she could say another word he'd swung back round again, reached under, and pressed the button.

CHAPTER 28

There was a sudden rumble under the surface and the metal steps began to vibrate. They all instinctively bundled back up onto the platform. The water began to churn and bubble and a circle of red lights around the submerged access panel began to blink.

'This is so LOUD,' cried Elena. 'We're going to be heard!'

'It's moving!' squeaked Tima, grabbing hold of their arms. 'It's rising up!'

She was right. Matt could see the metal dome slowly getting closer to the surface. He held his breath, mesmerized, as the dome breached the skin of the lake and broke through, sending out a small circular tidal wave. It rose up to the level of the steps and then stopped. The red lights blinked for a few more seconds and then turned green as the dome let out a hiss and a pop . . .

and then the wheel spun 360 degrees . . . and the hatch door slowly opened, easing up ninety degrees on a hinge.

Matt shoved the girls behind him as Lucky hopped into a niche in the bricks. He reached into his backpack for his baseball bat, and then realized he'd sharpened it into a stake and lost it in the graveyard after the struggle with Spin. He had no other weapon. He cursed aloud. How could he have been so stupid? There was a perfectly good wheel wrench in the back of the Ford which would have done. His bare fists might not be enough against whoever was coming up through that shaft. He clenched them anyway.

But nobody came out of the shaft. The bubbling, churning, and rumbling subsided and it simply stood there, open and waiting as the water slowly grew less agitated around it. The blue light shone from it in a soft vertical beam. No shadows or noise suggested anyone was climbing up to see who'd pressed the button.

'OK,' said Matt, at length. 'I'm going in. You two should probably wait here.'

'Yeah, right,' said Elena, and Tima snorted. No surprises there, then.

Matt went down onto the steps again and from there it was easy to reach across, grab the lip of the open hatch, and climb into it. There were metal rungs inside but the blue light was so bright he couldn't make out where they led. It couldn't be that far down, though, could it? The reservoir wasn't very deep. Taking a steadying breath and ordering his pulse to stop racing so fast, Matt climbed down to waist level and then beckoned

165

Tima across. As the girls followed on, he began to work his way steadily down the rungs. They were smooth and surprisingly warm under his fingers; perhaps the machinery which had pushed them up created heat.

Glancing down he could now make out a floor—some kind of pale silver metal. Aluminium, maybe. The blue glow was shining up from a line of lights set into the wall at ankle height. He reached the foot of the ladder in a few seconds and saw that the shaft simply twisted to a corridor leading in one direction, out across the bed of the reservoir as far as he could tell. A door with another submarine-style wheel on it was a short walk away. He waited until Elena and Tima had landed before motioning them to follow him.

'How far under the surface do you think we are?' whispered Elena. She sounded scared. Tima wasn't saying anything at all— and that meant she was definitely scared. Oddly, this made Matt feel more in control. If they were scared, he mustn't be. He was the oldest. And a boy. He wouldn't dare say that bit out loud, because Tima would instantly brand him as sexist but the point was, if people were younger than you, you had to step up. And if they were girls and you were a boy . . . well, same again.

He took a deep breath. 'About five metres, I reckon,' he whispered back. 'Do you want to go back? The hatch is still open. We could go back now and tip the police off and—'

'—let everyone know what we do at nights?' murmured Tima. 'No way. Keep going.'

'I think I heard stories about this,' Elena breathed, staring around. 'The guy who used to own the land around here was an old eccentric—really into science and experiments. He had all kinds of underground bunkers built in the fifties and sixties. This must be one of them. Only . . . an under *lake* bunker.'

'Doesn't look very 1950s to me,' said Tima.

'Well, no,' said Elena. 'But he could have been updating it over the years.'

Matt reached the door. He realized Lucky was on his shoulder again. 'You should go back,' he said to her. 'You don't need to come down here, you know.'

'Know,' she echoed. Or maybe she was arguing 'No', because she wasn't budging. He sighed. He was surrounded by feisty females. He reached for the wheel, grasped it, and turned. It moved with more ease than he was expecting, revolving silently, with little resistance. The door was oval, with a seal which gave a pop as he pushed it. Stepping up over its high lip, he walked into a wide, round room, suffused in blue light.

Where Liam Bassiter punched him in the face.

CHAPTER 29

Spin hated to behave like a needy boyfriend but he tried Elena's number again. Twice. After standing around in the wood in a most uncharacteristic state of uncertainty, he'd gone back home and picked up the landline phone once more. Again—voicemail. And then, ten minutes later, the same. He should have arranged to meet them tonight. Made a plan. Why had he been so vague? *Because you were scared and shaking and you had to get away before they noticed*, his inner voice pointed out. *You weren't capable of planning a sandwich.*

Where was she? Where were they all? And what were they doing?

'Are you OK?' Astrid stood in the kitchen, looking across the hall at him, brows drawn down in confusion. She knew he hardly ever made phone calls.

'Um . . . yeah,' he said. 'Just . . . calling this girl I know.'

The eyebrows shot up. 'A girl, eh?' She managed to fit seven different notes into those three syllables.

Spin sighed. 'Just a girl. A friend.'

'What girl is going to be up at this hour?' Astrid glanced at the kitchen clock which was showing 1.43 a.m. She took a quick breath. 'Oh . . . someone from the EPP support group? Have you been chatting online?'

'Someone . . . else,' he said. 'But she's not picking up so she's probably asleep . . . or busy.' Spin rarely lied to Astrid. He omitted to mention quite a lot . . . like his occasional break-ins. He almost never stole anything or left damage so he didn't consider these a crime; just entertainment.

'You should get a smart phone,' said Astrid. 'Join the twenty-first century.'

'Not my thing,' he said.

'Honestly, Spin, you're a real dinosaur!'

'I use the laptop,' he said. 'I just don't like social media. All those selfies and cat videos. It's puerile.'

'It's a way of connecting,' Astrid said, softly, going back to making coffee, 'with everyone else.'

But she didn't understand. Or maybe she did and that's what all the blood exchange stuff had been about. Her son was becoming too remote; too different; a distant satellite to others of his own age. 'I'm going out,' he said.

'Good,' she said back. 'Get out of my hair, dinosaur.'

For the second time that night, Spin walked out into the

woods. He stood, wondering what to do. Then he made his way to the canal. Aboard *The Nightjar* he lay flat along her gently curved roof and stared up into the starless gloom of the November night. The flat sky lit up green for a few seconds. Some fireworks warehouse had obviously been selling a job lot of green rockets at a discount this year.

Dammit. Where were they?

CHAPTER 30

It wasn't a hard punch—barely a slap. Liam staggered towards him, unbalanced by the effort, and collapsed in Matt's arms.

Tima stood frozen in the blue chamber, which was about four times the size of her bedroom and an extraordinary shape—like an upturned bowl. It was a dome, made of hundreds of thick hexagonal panes of glass set into metal—beyond the glass pressed the weight of millions of gallons of water. She noticed there were large white beanbags scattered around and three other figures lay in them. It was suffocatingly warm. Her head swam a little and she grabbed hold of Elena's arm.

'You . . .' Liam was muttering. '*You*?!' He swore in a low voice as he untangled himself from his enemy and slumped to the floor. 'I thought you were one of *them*. What the hell are *you* doing here?!'

Matt was staring, open-mouthed. Liam looked pale but not dead. He was dressed in a grey cotton jersey T-shirt and shorts, as were the other three figures on the beanbags, who were slowly getting up on their elbows and peering across at the commotion.

Matt knelt down next to Liam. 'Everyone thinks you're dead,' he said. 'The whole school got told in assembly. Elena went to your funeral.'

Liam looked baffled.

'*I* didn't lose any sleep about you, obviously,' Matt went on. 'But then we dug up your coffin and found bags of flour instead of a corpse.'

'We had a tip-off,' interjected Elena. 'We don't dig up coffins for a laugh.'

Liam stared across at her, recognition creeping across his narrow face. He sat up and took in a long, slow breath. 'They're . . . changing us,' he croaked. 'I think.'

Tima knelt down beside him and clutched his shoulder. 'Changing you, how? What have they done?'

'Nothing . . . I mean . . . they're just messing with the air,' he said.

'Who is?' asked Elena. 'Who brought you here?'

Liam let off a load of earthy descriptives for his captors.

'Yeah, we know *what* they are,' said Matt. 'But *who* are they?'

'That doctor from the hospital,' said Liam. 'Castle. And another guy . . . foreign.'

'Italian?' asked Tima. He shrugged.

'His name is Lazaro,' came another voice, and Tima looked up to see Megan getting out of her beanbag and wandering

172

across on unsteady legs. 'They drugged us and they brought us here. They say nobody's going to miss us.'

'But . . . *why*?' asked Tima, going to her and taking her warm, sweaty hand.

'Why won't anyone miss us?' Megan shrugged. 'Well, *they* think because we're in a home or fostered nobody will bother about us. But they're wrong! Stacey, our house parent at the home is lovely and she cares. My friend Ellie cares too. I will be missed,' she took a breath and gulped back a sob. 'I *will*.'

Tima and Elena glanced at each other and Elena moved over and put her arm around the girl's shoulders. 'Of course you will,' she said.

'But . . . you said they've faked our deaths?' asked Megan, beginning to cry. 'Is that true?'

Elena nodded. 'I'm sorry . . . but . . . yes. They filled coffins with bags of flour.'

'Do you know why they've brought you here?' asked Tima, trying to be gentle but desperate to know.

'They're selling us,' said Megan, with a sniff. 'That's why.'

'Who are they selling you to?' asked Elena.

Megan glanced around at the other captives. They all wore the same look; faces set like concrete. 'You mean *what* are they selling us to,' she said.

'Look—we can talk about all this later,' said Matt, hauling Liam up on to his feet. 'Let's get out of here!'

Unsteady as they all were, Tima expected them all to get up, ready and willing to escape. They didn't. Instead they looked at each other and dropped their eyes to the floor.

173

Liam shook his head at Matt. 'Birdbrain. You didn't even look behind you.'

Tima, Matt, and Elena slowly turned around. The door they had come through had vanished.

CHAPTER 31

Elena felt her knees buckle. A roaring sound went through her head and she sank down onto the floor. She was dimly aware of Matt charging at the wall and pummeling along its curve, trying to find the door, Lucky flapping around his head. It had a series of panels, identical. Any one of them could be the door. But none of them was giving in the slightest.

Elena moaned aloud. The fear flooding through her was only matched by her sense of idiocy. How could they have all been so *stupid*? One of them should have stood guard at the top of the hatch, another in the corridor, holding the door open. Why the hell had they all bundled in here without a backward glance? How incredibly dumb could you get?

She rolled onto her back and stared up . . . and felt her world tip and spin. The geodesic dome—she recognized the shape from a visit to bio-domes in Cornwall—arched out above them from the top of a tall curved concrete wall, panelled in white metal on its lower level, where Matt was still pummeling for an exit. Through the glass, beyond the distorted blue reflection of the room, she could clearly see the waters of the reservoir. It shouldn't be possible to make out anything, in the way you couldn't see out into the night from a brightly-lit room—and yet the water swirled and rippled past and she even caught sight of waving weed and the occasional fin and tail. She realized there was also lighting outside, deep in the bed of the lake; making it visible. The old landowner must have created this as some kind of underwater observatory. It was stunning but also disorientating.

'It's better if you don't look,' said a voice next to her, and a girl's face blocked her sightline. 'It makes you feel sick.'

Elena closed her eyes, took a deep breath, and sat up. The girl was pretty, with blue eyes and soft red hair which fell in disorganized ringlets to her shoulders. 'I'm Kacey,' she said. 'And this is Lewis.' A boy was kneeling nearby. His hair was a much darker red, and close cropped. His eyes were hazel green and watchful. 'He's been here the longest,' Kacey said. 'They got him first. He was sleeping rough, so he was easy.'

'What . . . is it . . . with the red hair?' Elena asked, trying to get a hold of her erratic breathing and not be sick with fright in front of them.

'They like red hair,' said Kacey. 'It's popular. They get paid more for redheads.' She gave a mirthless chuckle. 'Who knew? After all the ginger jokes, we're really *special*.'

'Who *are* they?' asked Tima, who was sitting nearby, hugging her knees to her chest. Behind her, Matt was sliding down the doorless wall and staring up at the underside of the reservoir, mouth agape.

'They're a bit like us,' said Kacey, with a gulp. 'But they're . . .'

' . . . twice our height,' supplied Lewis, with a twisted smile.

'And they only have three fingers,' said Kacey.

It sounded crazy to Elena. But crazy had been the new normal in her life for some time now. 'Are you saying they're . . . aliens?' she asked.

'Oh yeah,' said Lewis. 'They're very alien.' He picked at his nails.

'So . . . what do they want you for?' Tima said. 'Experiments?'

Kacey shook her head. 'I thought that too, but actually . . . no. They want us as . . . pets.'

'Pets?' breathed Elena. 'Oh my god. Spin was right.'

'They've been taking kids off Earth for years,' said Lewis. 'Centuries. Or so they say. They don't take babies, because babies can't survive the journey. You need to be at least eight—and under sixteen. They don't like them too old. They want us young enough to train.'

'Train? To do what?' asked Elena.

Lewis shrugged. 'I don't know. Sit. Stay. Roll over and beg.' He moved on to a new fingernail, his mouth a tight, straight line.

'Why are you all still here, then?' asked Matt. He was sitting next to Liam now, although he was doing his best not to look at his old foe.

'We're learning to breathe,' said Megan. 'They say the planet we're going to is quite like Earth but it has a slightly different mix of gases. And it's really hot. If they take human kids over too quickly, quite a lot of them have heart and lung failure. We have to acclimatize. So the air in here has been changing, slowly, since we got here. You're probably noticing it quite a lot, because you've just got here.' She glanced around at them all. 'Take it easy and don't move around too much. You'll feel really weird if you do.'

Elena was feeling really weird already. She closed her mouth and concentrated on taking long, slow breaths through her nostrils, trying to slow her panicky heartbeat as Megan went on.

'We've been getting shots too—immunizations against their diseases. And vitamin boosts. Lots of fizzy calcium drinks. They've got it all worked out. They know exactly what they're doing. Hey . . . isn't it nice to be wanted?' Tears suddenly began to leak down her face. 'I don't want to go,' she sniffed. 'I don't want to.'

'You're not going anywhere,' said Matt, fiercely. 'We came to get you out . . . and we will.'

There was a dry, cracked laugh. 'Yeah, right,' said Liam. 'How are you going to do that, bird boy? Is your little feathered friend going to peck an escape hole?'

Lucky was back on Matt's shoulder, her head drooping. He stroked her wings and stared back at Liam. 'We're going to work this out.'

'Face it, mate. You just screwed up. We're going to an alien world, like it or not. And now you're coming too.'

Elena realized something devastating. For the past few months she had grown used to feeling almost invincible. They had fought an underworld *god*—and saved Thornleigh from being wiped out by its voracious dark-light hunger. They'd helped track down deadly plants from another planet and saved Earth from unstoppable biological Armageddon.

But all these things they'd done because they were Night Speakers. Because they could call upon the astonishing power of the animal world to help them.

Now they were all entombed in a glass bowl, under water. How could she possibly get word to her foxes and squirrels and deer and all the other mammals who protected her . . . from here? How could Tima connect with her insects? How could Matt get any help beyond Lucky? At the head of a vast murmuration, Lucky was an amazing ally . . . but here, on her own . . . she was just one small bird. And she didn't look too good right now, clinging to Matt's shoulder, her beak agape and her wings tented out as she breathed fast and shallow, trying to lose heat.

Elena felt as powerless as a spider trapped under a glass.

CHAPTER 32

When the door finally reopened, easing out of the panels around it with a slight hiss, no alien came in. Instead a stockily-built woman with mousy hair entered, accompanied by Mr Castle from Thornleigh Hospital.

'We've been watching them for the last half an hour, on the cameras,' Castle was saying, flicking a glance across the three newest arrivals. 'Obviously they found out something they shouldn't.'

'Yeah—that you're not fit to call yourself a doctor!' snarled Matt, getting to his feet. 'You're some kind of psychopathic child slave trader.'

Castle shrugged. 'If you like. And while we're slinging insults, you're a grade A moron. All three of you are. Did you really think you could just walk into a state-of-the-art facility like this without being noticed?'

Matt realized it too and chose that moment to hurl himself at Castle. Castle took a head-butt to the chest but Matt got no further. The woman swiped out and struck an efficient blow to his temple. Matt went down as if he'd been hit by a truck. Elena gave a cry and dashed over to him, dropping to her knees. Tima just froze, her mind in free-fall. How were they going to get out of this? She sank to her knees, dizzy and weak.

'They can have these too, if they like,' said Castle, straightening his tie. 'They might not last very long; they've not been acclimatized, but we might pick up something for them. Maybe for dissection.'

'Hmmm,' said the woman. 'The girls are pretty. If only they were red. I could *make* them red. Of course, we can't guarantee them for a full lifespan; if they make it through they might last five years. Some buyers will take them for a discount.'

'And the boy?' asked Castle.

The woman shrugged. 'It can't hurt. I'll get enough dye for all three.'

'You can't be serious,' said Tima, her voice high and panicky. 'I mean . . . look at me! I'm from the Middle East! I'll look *ridiculous* with red hair!'

The woman stared at her and was about to say something when another person arrived in the doorway; it was Lazaro. Like Castle he wore a white lab coat. He was carrying a small red case. He made for Matt first, crouching over him and swiping Lucky aside as she fluttered pathetically, trying to guard her boy. Elena, still kneeling next to Matt, seemed unable to move, staring at the floor. Tima guessed she was trying to keep control of her stomach—the heat, the weird gas mix, and the swirling water above them made for a nauseous combination.

'So . . . I was right about you,' he said to Matt, smiling like a kindly uncle as he opened the case. 'You were talking my language. And listening to my language too, weren't you? A fluent Italian-speaking kid in Thornleigh. Who would expect that?'

Tima realized he was speaking Italian now. She understood it perfectly, of course. Before she could think better of it she spat back at him, in his own tongue: 'Your family would be ashamed of you, Lazaro. Do they know you've become a slave trader?'

'Oh ho! And you too!' he responded, glancing up at her. 'Are you all Italian?'

'Would it make a difference?' asked Elena, still looking at the floor.

'No, tesora, it wouldn't. You've made a very bad decision, coming here. I cannot un-make it for you. But at least you will have a chance. Your life will be very different . . . but not over. They treat their pets kindly on Rimagada.'

Tima struggled to her feet and crossed towards him. 'Don't do this,' she said, feebly. 'You don't need to do this. It's not too late. You haven't killed anyone. You haven't sent any of the kids off to this planet yet. You're better than this!'

He gave her a rueful grin. 'It's sweet that you think so,' he said, and stuck a needle into Matt. 'But I'm really not.' Elena screamed as he did the same to her, jabbing it into her shoulder.

Tima found herself being grasped by the mousy woman.

'Don't struggle,' she said, in her flat, nasal voice. 'I could kill you with my thumbs if I chose to.'

Then Lazaro jabbed Tima's shoulder too and the room became a blur and then darkened to nothing.

CHAPTER 33

Someone was watching. The prickly feeling at the back of his neck was never wrong. Spin sat up on the roof of *The Nightjar* and twisted around to look towards the bank. At first he saw nothing and then . . . there was movement. Twin white discs shone out of a patch of nettles. They blinked . . . and a fox walked out onto the canal path, staring right at him.

He held still, watching. He'd seen many foxes over the years and was often surprised by how bold they were. Most of them in this area had got used to his night-time prowling. He didn't bother them and they didn't bother him. But this one was familiar.

'Hello again, Elena's buddy,' he said. It didn't move. 'You tried to take a chunk out of my arm back in the summer,' he added. It opened its mouth, panting and letting its tongue ripple across its fangs for a moment and he could have sworn it was laughing at him. 'And you brought her to the graveyard, didn't you? You understood me.'

The fox closed its mouth and continued to stare at him. Spin stared back and then let out a frustrated: '*Whaaat*?'

The fox turned and walked away along the path, its tail held high, pointing its finely whiskered snout west. Then it paused and looked over its shoulder at him. Spin watched and waited. The fox came back and stared at him some more and gave a low growl.

'Look . . . I don't speak vulpine,' muttered Spin. 'I'm not Elena.'

The fox snapped its snout up at him at the mention of her name. It turned west again and once more walked the canal path, tail up. Then it looked at him once more and, if he wasn't imagining things, motioned sharply with its angular black nose, back in the same direction.

Spin slid onto the deck and stood up, peering at the creature. 'Are you asking me to take a walk with you?' The fox dipped its head. 'Why . . . are you taking me to Elena?' He felt a sudden fizz through his spine. 'Do you know where they all are?'

The fox suddenly went to the very edge of the bank and peered along the waterway. Then it turned, trotted to the aft of *The Nightjar*, and jumped lightly up onto the deck. Spin was taken aback. 'So what do you want? Am I meant to follow you? Or are you after a boat trip?'

In answer, the fox leapt onto the gently-curved roof and walked along it to the prow, where it stood, like a figurehead, staring straight ahead. Bemused, Spin fished in his trouser pocket and pulled out a bunch of keys. One of them was for the narrowboat engine. Shaking his head, he inserted the key and turned it. The motor coughed a couple of times and then puttered into life. He expected the fox to flee back to the bank and the woods at this point, but all it did was glance back at him, as if in approval, and then continue to stare straight ahead down the canal.

'O . . . K,' muttered Spin. 'If you say so. Let's go.'

He pushed the handle forward and steered the vessel gently away from the bank. 'Are you sure about this?' The fox only flicked its ears and lay down, still facing forward.

Spin flicked on the headlamp on the prow and it sent a wide, pale beam ahead of the vessel. Travelling in a narrowboat by night was against canal regulations in this area, but he was pretty sure there were no other boaters this far down to complain.

The ghostly white arrow of a barn owl swooped over his head. The fox glanced up at it, as it flew on down the canal, dead centre above the gently-lit water. Then the bird turned, flew back to just above him, turned again and flew on in the same direction.

If he wasn't mistaken, the animal world very much wanted to influence his plans tonight.

Spin took a deep breath and started to hum a little tune as he steered on, quietly carving a wake through the inky water. Well, it was better than waiting by the phone.

CHAPTER 34

Elena awoke on a white beanbag, to a smell like a public toilet. Groggily, she sat up and peered around. She was still in the underwater dome. Her hair felt damp. She brushed a strand of it off her face and realized it was a different colour. *Red*. That's what the smell was.

'Suits you,' said a quiet voice. It was Kacey. She was lying on a neighbouring beanbag. 'Not sure it works so well for your friends,' she said. 'Tima's skin tone doesn't really match it and Matt's has gone a bit purple.'

'Who did this?' breathed Elena.

'Edwina. She went and got some spray-on dye and did you all while you were out cold. Stinks, doesn't it?'

'Edwina,' echoed Elena.

'Yeah, the social worker from hell,' said Kacey. 'She's the one who started it all. She's the one who the aliens got to make the offers to Castle and Lazaro . . . and probably some guy at the undertakers. She's the fixer. The go-between. They're all being paid millions, apparently. I always thought Thornleigh was even more boring than King's Lynn. Turns out there's some kind of doorway from here to other planets—right here in Thornleigh. Who knew?'

'*We* knew,' said Elena. 'It's a cleftonique corridor.'

'What's that?' asked Kacey. 'And how do *you* know about it?'

'It's a kind of wormhole. It was opened earlier this year—by a different alien,' said Elena, battling a peculiar sleepiness which lay like a fire blanket over her insistent panic. 'Then another alien came through to catch the first one, to stop it terraforming Earth for another bunch of aliens.'

Kacey sat up and shook her head. 'Seriously?'

'Yeah,' said Elena. 'Seriously. And we know about it . . . because it created this kind of magnetic beam which goes back and forth through our bedrooms at the same time every night. It's turned us into insomniacs.' She could have added that it had made them multilingual across all human and animal life too, but stuck down here, trapped and possibly unable to ever speak to Velma and her other wild friends ever again, it seemed a bit pointless to mention it.

'So . . . Where is it? This corridor—wormhole thing?' asked Kacey. 'Have you seen it?'

'No,' said Elena. 'It's somewhere inside Leigh Hill, we think. That's what the second alien . . . the one we helped to arrest the first one . . . told us. We've looked for a way in but so far there's been only one cave and that's just a way down to the underworld. We blocked that off to stop a bad-tempered god eating the town.'

'OK,' said Kacey. She didn't look sceptical. Elena guessed her sceptometer had blown several days ago when she first found out about her one-way trip off Earth.

On the other side of her, Tima suddenly sat up, running her hands through her damp, newly-dyed hair. 'What have they done?' she murmured. 'I'm ginger!'

'You're more saleable,' grunted Matt, getting up and walking over to join them with Lucky huddled close into his neck. His hair was sticking up and a worrying shade of burgundy. 'Like a chocolate Labrador.'

'We've got to get out of here,' said Tima. She stood up, walked shakily to the edge of the chamber and pressed her palms and her forehead against one of the hexagonal glass panels. 'How did they even make this? Here in Thornleigh? It's like something out of a Bond film!'

Elena joined her, and Matt and Lucky soon arrived at her side as they all stared out into the dark, uplit waters of the reservoir. 'We've really messed up, haven't we?' Tima sighed.

'It's partly alien,' said Megan, coming over to join them. 'Apparently this has been here for decades but they've kind of souped it up with alien tech. They've sealed it properly, to stop any leaks—and they've pumped gases in, so we'll all get used to their atmosphere.'

'How do you know all this?' asked Elena.

'They showed us a video,' said Kacey. '*An Introduction to*

Rimagada. Like something they put on for you to watch at school.'

'What's it like?' asked Tima, still leaning against the glassy wall and staring up into the reservoir.

'It's . . . wet,' said Kacey. 'Boggy and steamy. Lots of alien insects and amphibians. They eat them. And algae. They eat a lot of algae.'

'There are volcanoes too,' said Megan. 'Loads of them. There's a lot of sulphur in the atmosphere.' She sighed and closed her eyes. 'I guess we'll get used to it . . . eventually.'

Elena gulped. 'Sulphur isn't good for you. I read a thing about sulphur mineworkers . . . they don't tend to live beyond thirty.'

'Nor will we,' said Megan. 'Life expectancy for a human pet is about fifteen years once you get there. Like a dog.'

'They told you this?' asked Tima, looking sick and scared. Elena reached over and squeezed her shoulder.

'Well, it's not in the *welcome to your new planet* video,' shrugged Megan. 'But we heard Edwina talking about it.'

'At least we'll never get old and wrinkly,' said Kacey, her eyes welling up.

Elena wasn't so sure about that. They might just age with great rapidity and end up looking eighty before they turned twenty-five.

'So have you actually *met* one of the aliens?' she asked.

'No,' said Megan. 'We've just seen a hologram of the one Edwina's trading with. They're like tall, thin humans. Apparently they can be kind . . .' She gulped.

'This isn't going to happen,' said Matt. 'They're not taking us.

We're not pets!'

Elena was impressed at how confident and steady he sounded. She wished she could believe him.

'Oh yeah?' came a familiar voice. Liam and Lewis had now joined their little huddle. Liam looked sharper now, than he had when they'd first arrived. 'You reckon you can stop them, birdbrain?!'

Matt swung around angrily but before he could get stuck into his old foe, Elena decided to take drastic action. With everything else they had to cope with, Liam Bassiter being . . . Liam Bassiter . . . was just too much. She stepped over to him and put her hands on his shoulders, looking directly up into his narrow, permanently suspicious eyes. Those eyes widened in surprise as she spoke softly to him. 'Liam,' she said. 'I'm really scared. Can you and Matt—please—just for now, stop getting at each other?'

Liam opened his mouth and then shut it. He looked absolutely astonished. She guessed that no girl had ever asked him for anything. 'If we work together,' she went on, 'we might find a way out of here. Do you think . . . ?'

He nodded slowly, blinking, and she felt the fear in him. 'Thank you,' she said. She let go of him and glanced across to Matt, who looked wary and tense. She locked eyes in a way that left him in no doubt of how angry she would be if he messed up this fragile moment. 'You too, Matt. Please.'

He nodded and rolled his eyes. 'All right.'

'Right then,' said Liam. 'What's the plan, bird—I mean . . . *Matt*?'

Lewis cut in, in a low voice: 'Look . . . any plan we make, it'd better be a quiet plan,' he said, in what sounded like a Yorkshire accent. 'We're being watched and listened to all the time, you know.' He waved his arm around vaguely because there were no obvious cameras on show.

'How long have we got?' asked Matt, dropping his voice. 'Before they take us? And will they be taking us up out of here and driving us to the place where they come through?'

'You have two hours and twenty-eight minutes.' They all spun around to see Edwina standing in the doorway. 'You go before dawn. You won't be going out on Earth again. There's a short range transporter beam which will jump you to the planet exit point. Then you'll exit Earth from there. You may as well get used to the idea. You're going to have an amazing adventure on a new planet—many people would give their eyeteeth to swap places with you.'

'Until they found out about the lifespan,' said Matt, squaring up to her. 'I don't think you'd fancy it much, would you?'

'I'm not young or cute enough,' she said, with a smirk. 'But don't worry—the Rimagadans treat their pet humans very well. You'll be well fed and looked after. They like to cuddle. Try not to screw up your pretty little faces when they do; they don't like that. Be affectionate back and everyone will be happy.'

'Happy?' Elena stared at her, aghast. 'You've done this before, haven't you?'

Edwina smirked. 'I've rehomed forty-six children in the past three years.'

'*Rehomed*? Is that what you call it?' Elena felt fury fizzing through her. She let go of Tima and stepped towards the social worker, wondering if she would get a chance to slap her across that smug face before she was disabled. Matt looked as if he was thinking the same.

'Look, sweetheart,' said Edwina, 'I'm not talking about spoilt brats like you. I'm talking about kids who nobody wants; runaways, abused or neglected at home or shoved around the care system; kids who will never fit in. I have *rescued* them from miserable, hopeless lives, and sent them to homes where they will be adored.'

'In return for a big fat payment,' muttered Matt.

'How did you even meet these aliens?' asked Elena.

'I've met all sorts,' said Edwina, shrugging. 'There are more alien things going on around this planet than you could guess at. Anyway,' she gave them a sickly smile, '*children*, I didn't come here for a chat. I came here to tell you that you need to lie down again and relax. Passing through the corridor will be much easier on you if you don't fight it. Go with it, and it'll just sting a bit. Fight it, and you'll feel like you're being sandblasted. Quantum entanglement is brutal if you struggle. It'll take you days to recover.'

'*Relax*? Are you kidding?!' snorted Matt. He ran at her then but she sidestepped him easily and then cackled as he stumbled and fell.

'*You* are going to have a very bad time of it,' she sniggered. 'But you brought this on yourself, nosing around. I have no sympathy for you.'

She stepped back through the open door and it vanished,

leaving only a smooth white panel.

Elena felt a wave of hopelessness wash over her. She noticed that Tima was lying down at the far edge of the floor, up against the glass dome wall. Her hands were pressed to one of the hexagonal panes as she gazed out into the watery world beyond. Desperation chased the hopelessness and Elena sank down onto the floor herself. She checked her watch. It was half past four in the morning. Daylight would break around seven. But it looked like none of them would be here to see it.

CHAPTER 35

Instinct told Spin to switch off the headlamp as he reached the reservoir. He killed the engine too and allowed the boat to drift as his night vision slowly kicked in. He'd spent a lot of time in dark, wooded areas and his nocturnal eyes were exceptional, so the pale shimmer of the lake was soon revealed to him. It was a long, kidney-shaped expanse of water, lined with trees on all sides except at its western edge, where the jagged, dark skyline dipped abruptly to a flat line of concrete—half a kilometre of reservoir wall which hung above the north western end of Thornleigh, silently shouldering the pressure of several million gallons of water.

At the prow, the fox sat up and glanced back at him questioningly. 'Look—*you* brought me here!' Spin muttered. 'So don't look at me like that. *I* don't have all the answers. Where is Elena? It's a big lake and there are lots of trees, Foxy. So I'm going to need a clue.'

He expected the fox to stand up and point its nose helpfully in one direction, but it didn't. It stood, circled, peered over into the water and then circled again. It was the furry embodiment of uncertainty. Then, suddenly, it tensed. Its ears pricked forward and its snout rose into the air, pointing towards the thickly wooded reaches of southern bank.

Spin pushed the tiller to the right and the boat slowly turned left and drifted towards the bank. Spin considered switching the engine back on, but instantly rejected that notion when he caught sight of a light through the trees. He couldn't risk attracting attention. Happily, the chilly night breeze was carrying the vessel in the right direction, so he simply steered it past some bullrushes and up against a stretch of shore edged with old railway sleepers. A small willow tree bent over the water and provided both shelter from casual view and a handy low branch to tie up to.

As soon as they had docked, the fox leapt onto the bank and paced around agitatedly while Spin tied up, then, the moment he stepped onto the land, the fox shot away in the direction of the light. Spin sighed and broke into an almost silent sprint along the compacted earth path that circled the reservoir. He guessed there must be some old cabin out here that Castle was using to contain the not-dead kids before he sold them on for parts or slavery or whatever. Had the others found it already, with help from all their animal mates? If so, what was Foxy doing here with him instead of helping Elena?

Of course, the obvious answer was that Elena was in trouble and this was why he'd been led here. Spin felt a peculiar rush of . . . what? Anxiety? Excitement? Confusion? He'd spent so long *being* the menace, it was pretty weird to be called upon to help fight another menace. It wasn't the first time, either, this year. He was letting his reputation down. This couldn't go on.

He saw a flash of the white tip of fox tail ahead in the trees—and further on, a chink of light through the foliage. Was that a car? He slowed and went into full stalker mode, rolling his feet in their soft-soled leather boots and quietening his breathing. Over the past few years he had perfected this. Surprise was one of his most important tricks. The fox had slowed too. He caught up with it, crouching in the shadows, at the edge of a gravelly clearing where two cars were parked; a red Ford Focus and a black BMW. The Ford was dark but the BMW was lit up inside and a man in white was sitting in the driver's seat, looking into a case of some kind. The driver's door was ajar, as if he was about to get out.

Spin grinned to himself. Here was Castle. All alone in the night. Undoubtedly up to no good. He glanced at the fox, drew in a long, contented breath, exhaled luxuriously, and said: 'Enter . . . the vampire . . .'

CHAPTER 36

If she could see them, then she guessed they could see her. Tima lay against the glass and stared through it, doing her best to block out everything behind her; to focus on nothing but the watery world just a few centimetres away from her face.

On the other side of the glass six or seven tiny, multi-legged creatures were dancing. They looked a bit like centipedes with their long, segmented bodies and fine antennae. They were, of course, freshwater shrimps; the insects of the water world. At first they had just clustered there as if by chance. Then Tima realized they were moving in a slow circle, following each other, head to tail. This was something she'd seen before—in her insects. One of the first things she had noticed, when she'd just become a Night Speaker but didn't yet know it, was the way insects were communicating with her in patterns . . . moving in ways they never normally would.

She felt her heart give a little lurch. *Can you see me?* she sent to them, hardly daring to hope. At once they all turned their bodies 360 degrees against the glass and then continued to follow each other in the wider circle. Tima let out a long breath. She considered calling Matt and Elena over to see it, but then thought better of it. They were all being closely monitored inside this dome. But maybe what was happening outside wasn't being monitored quite so closely. She wanted it to stay that way.

We can't get out, she sent. *We're in big trouble. Can you help us?* The shrimp circled on for a while and then spun individually again. More arrived at the party, suddenly streaming across the glass from all directions, to join the circle, adding further rotating layers to it.

Tima sat up and stretched and then reached out to touch Elena's foot. Her friend was lying nearby, staring blankly across the floor. She glanced over at Tima with a sad smile. There had been much whispered discussion of escape for some time after Edwina had left, but none of them had been able to concoct a workable plan. First Elena and then Matt had retreated into their own thoughts. Tima had never joined the discussion in the first place. She had been shrimp-watching the whole time.

Tima flicked her fingers discreetly, calling Elena across. As her friend arrived, she whispered: 'Don't say anything and don't stare too hard, but . . . look.'

Outside the shrimp dance had evolved to a full festival of sub-aquatic invertebrates. Tima could recognize crayfish and water fleas but there were other scurrying, leggy beings which she couldn't identify. And now they were being joined by tiny fish . . . darting in and out of the circles, making no attempt to snap up the tinier creatures which would normally be their prey; focusing entirely on the dance.

Elena stared out, her eyes widening.

'Try to act normal,' murmured Tima.

Elena glanced at her. 'We're prisoners in a submerged biosphere, trapped by alien tech and about to be transported to a new planet . . . what would pass for normal?'

Tima sat up and turned away from the wildlife circus. 'They know we need help,' she said, quietly. 'They want to help. I'm just not sure how they can.'

Matt crawled over to them. He glanced at the scene behind Tima and Elena and then studiedly looked away again, getting the message. 'We can still reach them,' he whispered, eyes alight.

'Yes . . . but how can they help?' asked Elena. 'They can't reach us, can they?'

'And if they could break through,' sighed Tima, 'we'd probably all drown.'

A sudden flare of green light went off, rippling through the water outside for a microsecond.

'Oh god,' said Kacey. 'It won't be long now.'

'What is that?' asked Matt. 'What's that green light? We thought it was fireworks.'

Kacey shook her head. 'It's alien tech. Every time Edwina comes through the . . . space portal or whatever it is . . . everything lights up green. She's powering it all up to send us out.'

The door appeared a moment later and Edwina and Lazaro strode in. Edwina was holding what looked like a glass prism in her palm, addressing the gangly, holographic figure of what could only be her alien counterpart.

' . . . within the hour?' she was saying.

'Yes,' came a crackly response—a clipped, flat voice from another world. 'The shutdown is imminent on the other side. This is the last shipment we can make for the foreseeable future. Time is running out. Where is Castle?'

'He went to the car to get some inhalers,' said Lazaro, pulling on the collar of his lab coat. 'The extra kids will need them on the other side. You won't be able to sell them if they're coughing and wheezing. He should be back any minute.'

'You seem anxious,' it said. 'Your heart rate is accelerated.'

'We're new to this,' Castle replied. 'Edwina's done it all before but we haven't. We're also . . . concerned . . . about whether our involvement in this might come out. There was another one, you see . . .'

'Another one?'

'What other one?' demanded Edwina. 'You didn't say anything to me about another one?'

'These three,' Lazaro indicated Tima, Elena, and Matt, 'were at an event in Thornleigh yesterday afternoon. They overheard a conversation I was having with Castle . . . that's how they knew something was going on. They were friends with that one,' he pointed to Liam, who was lying on one of the beanbags, drowsing. 'And we think they checked out his grave . . . got suspicious. Then they somehow followed us up here . . . we still don't know how.'

The alien didn't sound troubled. 'They will be gone from your world in less than an hour,' it said. 'Where is the problem?'

'Yes . . . it's just . . . there was another one with them yesterday; a boy who was being treated at the hospital where we harvested three of the others. He's still out there. He might make our lives . . . *awkward* . . . when this is all over.'

The alien did not respond.

'And if you want to use our services *again* one day,' said Lazaro, sounding slightly testy now, 'it will be easier if we're working at our new posts in Scotland rather than locked up in prison!'

The alien gave a grunt of understanding. 'I see. This other one. He lives in Thornleigh, yes?'

Lazaro nodded.

'Do you or Castle live in Thornleigh?'

'No,' said Lazaro. 'We live elsewhere.'

'Does anybody you care about live in Thornleigh?'

Tima felt a chill as Lazaro stared at the being in the prism, his brows first drawn together and then lifting as he took in the meaning of this question. 'No,' he said. 'Nobody. And Castle and his wife live an hour west of here.'

'And you, Edwina?' the alien added.

The social worker smiled thinly. 'There's nobody I care about in this *country*,' she said.

'Then your problem is easily solved,' said the alien. The room abruptly turned red and began to pulse.

Lazaro jumped and looked around, visibly unsettled. 'Do not

be alarmed,' said the alien. 'I have just set a countdown. You'll be gone long before it ends. You will be safe to move on to your Scottish hospital without fear of discovery and retribution.'

'What . . . what will happen?' breathed Lazaro.

'There will be a big distraction. A few missing children will no longer be significant,' said the alien, with a ghastly grey-toothed smile. 'When the countdown ends, the technology we have installed will vaporize itself. We never leave a trace of our work. The shockwave will demolish both the dome and the reservoir wall. The town will be flooded. Your troublesome boy will be drowned along with the rest of them.'

CHAPTER 37

'I know. I *know*, Selina. But they're short-staffed and I can't get away for another hour or so.' Castle was having a hard time of it on his mobile phone. Spin hung above the car, suspended from a sturdy branch, perfectly still. It was one of his best tricks, the stillness. He could gather the gloom around himself in a protective cloak and people never saw him, even when he was just a hand's reach above them. People were very obtuse. Even the Night Speakers, with all their superpowers, rarely knew when he was stalking them.

'I will be home for breakfast,' Castle went on. 'Then I'll have to get some sleep. I know. I *know*. Yes. Yes, I will. I promise. Yes. OK. OK. Love you too . . .' The phone pipped and the call ended. ' . . . You shrew,' concluded Castle. 'Wish I could send *you* to an alien planet.' He cursed and switched off the gadget.

Castle clambered out of the BMW, bringing the red plastic case with him. He shut the door, locked the car, and then got a faceful of gravel as he was flattened by the blunt strike of an assailant from above.

He had no time to make any sound other than an abrupt wheeze as the air was knocked out of him. Spin rolled him over onto his back and mantled the man with his open, red-lined coat, the way a falcon mantles its prey.

Castle stared at him in shock, mouth agape, round eyes peering up through thin round lenses. 'Wha . . . what?' he puffed.

'Remember me?' said Spin, pinning the man's wrists to the ground just beyond his balding head. 'The vampire?'

Castle gurgled in confusion, so Spin squeezed the button just inside his left sleeve and a ghostly blue light shone up from his collar, marking out his features in true horror movie style. He grinned widely, allowing his sharpened canines to show.

'Cr—Crispin Taylor?' the man croaked. Then he seemed to gather his wits just slightly. 'What . . . what are you doing here? You shouldn't be out so soon. You're sick!'

'Oh no, *you're* sick,' said Spin, his knee firmly planted on the man's heaving chest. 'What a sick, sick little plan you cooked up with that Italian morgue monkey.'

'I don't know what you mean,' rasped Castle, trying to wrench his wrists free. 'Crispin . . . you're delirious. I think you're having a reaction to the drugs. Let me get up. Let me help you.'

'You can help me,' agreed Spin. 'Your help is what I'm counting on, Mr Castle.' He leapt to his feet and allowed the man to get up. Castle glanced around, straightening his glasses and seeking an escape route.

'Trust me,' said Spin, the collar light still eerily picking out his features. 'There's no point in running. You won't get far before I catch you and then I'll be cross. I bite when I'm cross. Save your neck. Tell me where I can find my friends. You know the ones. Elena, Tima, and Matt—you saw them with me at the Winter Fair.'

The glitter in his eyes showed Spin that Castle knew exactly who he was talking about . . . and where they were. Also that his brain was in overdrive, trying to think of a way out of his predicament.

'Fine,' he said, with a short shake of the head. '*Fine*. I met your stupid friends. They followed me here with some crazy ideas about some kind of plot to kidnap sick kids.'

'Crazy? So what would *you* call it?' Spin stood still but his every nerve and sinew was ready to spring.

'I wouldn't call it *anything*!' blustered Castle. 'It's nonsense. I'm a respected paediatrician, for God's sake!'

'So what's a respected paediatrician doing up here in the dead of night?' queried Spin.

'I was . . . fishing!' Castle shrugged. 'I like to come night fishing. It's a great way to de-stress.'

'That's not what you told Selina,' pointed out Spin. He was enjoying this; he couldn't help himself.

Castle goggled at him for a moment.

'And it's an interesting angling outfit,' added Spin. 'A white lab coat. Where are your rods?'

'Set up . . . further along the bank,' snapped Castle. 'I can show you!'

'Ah, but what about my three troublesome friends? Did they disturb your trout tickling? Did you ask them to sit and watch your bait tin while you came back to the car?'

'Yes. As a matter of fact I did,' said Castle. 'One of them was having an asthma attack . . . the little girl . . . and I have some inhalers here!' He picked up the plastic case and opened it with a self-righteous flourish. It was filled with an assortment of inhalers.

'Tima had an asthma attack?' said Spin, rubbing his chin and frowning. 'Strange. I never knew she had weak lungs.'

'Well she does,' said Castle, stomping away along the path. 'She had a panic attack . . . something fell on her head from a tree. A big spider or something. She had hysterics and started hyperventilating. You know what little girls are like with spiders. Come on—I'll take you to her!'

'A spider, eh?' said Spin. 'Oh yes . . . I know what Tima's like with spiders.'

'Yes. Well. She's in a bad way. The others are looking after her. She's very scared. I need to get back to them.' He fumbled with a torch, got the beam trained along the uneven path ahead, and started walking with the case tucked under one arm.

Spin sprang after him, highly amused.

'So . . . remind me . . . what crazy plot did they accuse you of?'

'It's just nonsense. You young people all watch too much TV.'

'Go on . . . tell me what they said.'

'Something about those children who died last week not really being dead,' said Castle, keeping his eyes ahead and his torch beam low along the ground. Spin could see him surreptitiously feeling for his mobile phone in his pockets as he scuttled along. 'You were there for some of it—you can back me up. Those kids tragically died on the ward.'

'I was there,' said Spin. 'I remember hearing things.' He squeezed Castle's phone, safe in his own pocket. 'Where exactly is your fishing camp?'

Castle waved vaguely along towards the western shore where the dark woodland gave way to the bright gleam of the reservoir wall.

'Do you often come up here?' Spin asked. 'In the dark, in your white coat?'

'I have a *very stressful job*,' puffed Castle, feeling in his trouser pockets now, getting desperate.

Not as stressful as it's about to get, thought Spin.

CHAPTER 38

The flashing red light didn't do anything to relax the human pets. All seven of them stood around, staring at each other after Edwina and Lazaro had left the room.

'It said . . . it said the valley would be flooded,' gulped Elena. 'This whole place is going to explode and blow out the reservoir wall and millions of gallons of water are going to hit Thornleigh.' She shook her head, tears welling in her eyes. 'My mum's down there.'

Matt nodded grimly and put his hand on her shoulder. 'Mine too,' he said.

Tima shook her head. 'We should never have come here. If they didn't know we'd found out about them, they'd never be flooding the town. What have we done?'

'Well, they'd probably vaporize all this anyway,' said Kacey.

'They're not going to leave any alien tech in the lake for anyone to find, are they?'

'No,' came a harsh voice. Edwina was back, appearing once again from that unsettling doorway which arrived and vanished without warning, carrying a pile of grey material. 'They normally leave no trace of their tech behind but they destroy it silently with acids over a couple of hours rather than blow it up. So yes—if you want to get the guilts, it is your fault that most of your town's about to be swept away by a flood disaster.'

'And you don't care about that?' demanded Elena. 'Thousands of people . . . dead; swept away, drowned, buried in rubble. That's all right by you, is it?'

Edwina shrugged. 'Stuff happens. People die.'

Matt felt cold rage ripple through him. Lucky, on his shoulder, shivered in sympathy. The urge to attack this callous woman was incredibly strong, but he was so weak and disorientated by the red flashing light and the gas mix in the chamber. The blow on his temple still pulsed with pain.

'You,' said Edwina, pointing to Matt, Elena, and Tima. 'I need you in these clothes. Now.' She flung the grey material at them and Matt saw it was the same T-shirt and shorts outfit as the others were wearing. 'And don't let that bird poo on them. You need to look clean and presentable. The rest of you,' she went on, staring around at the other four. 'I need you in the wiping chamber. Come with me.'

'What's the wiping chamber?' Tima asked.

'You'll find out soon enough,' said Edwina. 'You'll be in next. Get a move on, all of you, unless you want to be here still when this thing blows up.'

Liam, Lewis, Kacey, and Megan trooped silently after Edwina. They looked passive and broken. Matt had never seen Liam accept authority like this before, without a snigger or a curse. It was peculiar and scary.

Once the others had gone—through a different door in the curved white wall—Matt, Elena, and Tima stared around at each other. 'I'm not putting these on,' muttered Matt.

'Put them *on*,' came an accented voice, from speakers hidden around the room. 'Or I'll have to pump in some gas, drop you where you stand, and come and dress you like a baby.'

Matt told Lazaro exactly what he could go and do with himself. But then he sighed, stooped down and gathered up the clothing. They all faced away from each other as they got out of their own stuff and into the shorts and T-shirts.

'We have to do something,' said Elena, once she was outfitted in the grey. 'Look! They know we need help!'

Outside was a maelstrom of churning water and it was filled with underwater wildlife. The tiny creatures had been joined by fish—carp, trout, pike, eels. They were thronging the water on the other side. One or two of them smashed against the glass and Matt thought he could even *hear* the thuds.

'Can they . . . can they break through?' Tima looked both hopeful and scared. 'If they do . . . can we escape?'

Matt shook his head. 'We're underwater . . . I don't know how far down. The lake would just fall on top of us.'

'Yes . . . But . . .' Elena pressed her hands against the glassy wall. 'If it did . . . if this thing collapsed *before* they could

211

vaporize it, it might be better for Thornleigh. If it's already smashed up when they vaporize it, the explosion won't be so big, will it?'

There was a definite thud as a massive fish with scary teeth—a pike, Matt thought—struck the dome.

'So . . . we might not survive,' said Matt. 'But Thornleigh would.' He shivered, imagining the water cascading down on top of them all through the smashed dome. 'Do we . . . do we ask them for help? To break through?'

'It might not work,' said Elena. She slapped her palm on the glass. 'But we can't let thousands of people die just because of us; just because we were too stupid to take care of ourselves.'

Tima nodded. She stepped up beside Elena, pressed her palms to the glass, and closed her eyes. Matt did the same. *Help us*, he sent. *Please. Do everything you can to smash this thing. Break it up. It's going to kill everyone we love . . . and most of you too . . . if you don't kill it first.*

'What the hell is that?' Lazaro was in the room behind them. He was clutching a phone in one hand and looking sweaty and agitated.

They turned to look at him and Matt took some small pleasure from seeing his shock. 'That,' he said, 'is the cavalry. They're breaking in.'

Lazaro gaped at him and then back out at the swirling mass of aquatic life, pounding and scraping against the dome. Matt was pretty sure there were some otters out there now; he could see flashes of fur and claws. The noise was rising and he could almost feel the pressure building as the sphere was attacked relentlessly from the far side.

'*Che diavolo . . . ?*' said the Italian, lapsing into his own language as he tried to make sense of this shift in events.

Matt followed him into his mother tongue. 'You wondered how we all spoke your language? Well, that's nothing. We're Night Speakers and we speak *any* language. Including animal language. We can communicate with all of them.' He waved to the hordes now crashing into the biosphere with incessant determination. 'And they understand everything we're asking them to do . . . and why we're asking it.'

'We're not going to let you drown Thornleigh,' said Elena. 'If there's nothing left to explode when that countdown ends, there'll be no big blast and the reservoir wall won't be smashed.'

Lazaro closed his eyes for a moment and raked his hand through his hair. '*Questo è folle!*' he said, his eyes travelling the scene outside and blinking with fear. 'If those things rupture this sphere, we'll all die. *You* will die. Do you know how much water there is up there?' He pointed to the lake surface.

'Better get them to stop that countdown and let us go, then,' said Tima.

Lazaro rolled his eyes. 'There is NO WAY that can happen, now. You're going to Rimagada. Accept it. There's no way to stop it.' He looked at his watch. 'Anyway, you'll be wiped in the next ten minutes and then you won't care either way.'

'Wiped?' Matt stepped forward and had the satisfaction of seeing Lazaro step back. 'What do you mean, wiped?'

Lazaro pulled some kind of needle pen out of his pocket and held it out in his fist. 'Stay away or you'll get a dose of this,' he said. 'It's a nerve agent. Agonizingly painful!'

'Tell us,' said Elena. 'What is "wiping"?'

'It's a memory cleaner,' said Lazaro. 'Alien technology. They wipe out all your memories; everything but the most basic cognitive functions. Like a hard reset on your mobile phone. It's kinder. You won't miss home because you won't remember it. It helps you to bond with your new owners. Makes you . . . quiescent.'

Matt felt his jaw drop. This nightmare just kept getting worse.

'Look,' said Lazaro, glancing nervously again at the water wall after a huge thud from an eel which had to be two metres long, 'I never signed up for this. I didn't want to cause mass death and destruction. I just wanted to give a new life to a handful of kids who'd been dumped by the system. They get love and care in this new place. It's not all bad . . . It's an amazing adventure.'

'Yeah. With your personality wiped away and your life span cut down to a quarter,' said Matt.

This time Lucky couldn't sit and bear his rage. She flew right at Lazaro's face, managing to scratch him across the cheek before he bashed her away. She landed in a heap of feathers on the floor and Matt gave a cry and ran to gather her up.

When he looked up again, Lazaro had gone. Then the man's stressed voice emerged from the hidden speakers. 'You're going to be wiped. Make your peace with it. Afterwards everything will be fine. Fine.' Then he clearly forgot to switch off the intercom, because they heard him mutter: 'Where the hell is

Castle?' Then they heard a few beeps from his mobile phone and his frustrated hiss to whoever had picked up: 'Where the hell are you?' before the intercom was closed down.

They turned back to the water wall, mesmerized. It was like some incredible animated tapestry. There was no longer a square inch of it without some kind of animal life attacking.

'It's strong,' said Elena. 'I don't know if they can do it. Remember it's been strengthened by the aliens.'

'Edwina,' said Tima. 'She said their tech gets dissolved in acid.'

'What kind of acid?' said Matt. 'We don't know. It could be alien acid. And anyway . . . whatever it is, we don't have any.'

'No . . . we don't,' said Tima, looking thoughtful in the red flashing light. 'But I know who does . . . if they could just get here . . .'

CHAPTER 39

Spin felt something buzz in his palm as he watched Castle
stumbling ahead of him, ever more frantically rummaging in his
pockets. He glanced down at the phone and saw a call coming
in: *LAZARO*.

'Is this what you're looking for?' he asked, holding it up.

Castle gaped at him, dropped the case and the torch, and
made a grab for the phone. Spin collected the man's hand in his
cupped palm, twisted his arm in a violent corkscrew, flipped him
and dumped him back on the floor. He settled his knee against
the dazed doctor's throat while he took the call.

'Where the hell are you?' hissed a voice with an Italian
accent.

'On my way,' puffed Spin, doing a fair impression of Castle,
running. 'Got delayed.'

'Well hurry up! The alien has set off a countdown and this whole place is going to vaporize in twenty minutes! We have to get these damn kids off this planet and get ourselves away from here before that happens. The reservoir wall is going to fail in the shockwave—and the whole town will be flooded.'

Spin took a moment to absorb this news, while holding his knee in just the right place to keep Castle's harsh gasps from turning to shouts. 'I lost my torch,' he hissed. 'I need you to shine a light so I can get to you.'

There was a volley of angry Italian and then Lazaro said: 'Fine. I'll go up to the platform and shine a light through the door. As soon as you see it, start running. I don't like this. At all. We need to get the inhalers in, load the kids' lungs up with salbutamol and send them on their way. I want *out* of this place . . . five minutes ago!'

'Shine the *light* then!' hissed Spin.

'On it now!' The call ended and Spin put the phone in his pocket.

'Interesting,' he said to Castle.

He eased his knee up enough for the man to splutter back at him: 'Money. I can give you money. Thousands . . . hundreds of thousands. I can cut you in on the deal. They're just kids nobody wants. They're going to a better place.'

'Isn't that what they say at funerals?' asked Spin. He allowed Castle to get up again, panting and dishevelled, before he raised one hand and, with expert angle and velocity, dropped him. Then, bending over, he tugged the white lab coat off.

In the trees along the bank, a short walk from the reservoir wall, a torch beam began to wave up and down.

'*Coming*,' sang Spin, and hopped over Castle's body.

CHAPTER 40

They would have put up a fight but for the Taser. When Edwina returned to the chamber she was armed with a state-of-the-art device.

'You may have put the wind up that dumb Italian,' she said. 'But don't think you're getting one over on me.' She barely glanced at the animal frenzy beyond the water wall. 'Set that bird on me and it'll be fried.'

Matt whispered to Lucky and she flew to the far side of the room, landing on the floor as she could find no perch. 'When the door opens,' Matt said, 'fly out. Get back up through the hatch and fly home.'

Lucky appeared to shake her feathered head. 'I mean it!' Matt said, a catch in his voice. Tima felt her eyes well up. Matt was trying to say goodbye. 'Go as soon as you can,' he instructed.

'I mean it. I care about you too much to take you any further with me. Go.'

'Care about you,' echoed Lucky, and Tima's tears spilled over.

'Right,' said Edwina, briskly. 'Come with me. You've got to be wiped.'

They stood, motionless. Tima tried to convince herself that this wasn't real. It couldn't be. This couldn't possibly happen to her.

Edwina pushed a button on the Taser and they heard it give a whine as it charged. 'This doesn't just hurt like hell,' said Edwina. 'It also makes you lose bladder control. If you want to pee your pants first, before being left here incapacitated, while this whole place explodes around you, you can do that in 5—4—3—2—'

They got moving. Elena took her hand and Matt was close behind. Tima glanced at them both and tried to commit them ... all that they were to her ... to memory. After everything they'd been through together it seemed impossible that in a few minutes she might be staring blankly at their faces and remembering nothing at all.

They entered another room. It was long and narrow and had a series of metal cubicles with stools in each.

Tima suddenly realized the other four were here. They were sitting, cross-legged, at the far end of the room, on a large oval platform. It had a dozen circles across it on the floor, each mirrored above on a low ceiling. Liam, Lewis, Kacey, and Megan were sitting on some of the circles in a column of green light. They were silent, their eyes wide and empty. They did not seem in any way nervous. They did not seem in any way anything.

CHAPTER 41

Spin reached the source of the light and found it was a small brick hut built onto the shore of the reservoir. Around the back of it, through a tangle of recently-trodden brambles and nettles, a door was open, light spilling out of it. A hand was waving a torch up and down with increasing agitation.

Spin ducked behind a thicket of holly trees and shrugged himself into the lab coat. It wasn't going to fool anyone for very long but it might give him a few seconds' worth of information.

'What's going on down there?' he yelled out, as he approached the back of the brick hut. He kept his voice low and gruff and hoped it would still pass for Castle's.

'I don't like it,' hissed his companion from the doorway. 'Those kids who followed us up here—there's something really weird about them. Look at the lake!'

Spin glanced back towards the lake as he climbed awkwardly across the brambles. Four or five metres out from the bank the water was churning. A widening circle of frothing, choppy waves was breaking the calm surface. 'What's that?' he grunted, taking the opportunity to turn his face away from Lazaro and hold off the moment of discovery a little longer.

'There's some kind of attack going on . . . against the dome. These kids say they can communicate with animals! They've got every bit of pond life in the reservoir head-butting the dome!'

Spin grinned into the darkness. 'That's not possible!' he grunted. It was. He'd seen similar things before.

'Well you should take a bloody look!' snapped the Italian. He sounded severely rattled. If he knew what Spin knew about the Night Speakers, he'd be a lot more rattled. 'Where the hell have you been, anyway?! You should have been back fifteen minutes ago! Have you got the inhalers?'

'Yes.' Spin turned around, holding the red case up in front of his face. He stepped into the doorway. The man had his back to him, already running down some concrete steps. Spin left the door ajar, pulling some of the vegetation from outside into the crack. He had years of burglary experience and knew never to shut a door behind him.

'Get a move on! We've only got fifteen minutes before the countdown ends. We have to get the last three wiped, then get them all onto the transporter bay.'

Spin trod carefully down behind Lazaro. There was a sea of blackness travelling the steps. The blackness did not cross his footsteps, as if it knew precisely where he was about to tread, and he took care not to interfere with it. Blackness was very much his ally.

Here in close quarters he could no longer risk talking to Lazaro. There was no way he'd pass for a 40-something paediatrician if he could be properly heard. He made a general grunting noise and followed on, preparing for the moment when Lazaro turned back and saw him.

At the foot of some concrete stairs, a short way out from a platform that hung over the water, Spin saw a strange circular hatch, breaching the surface of the lake, ringed with flashing red lights.

'It's a red flashing hell down here,' Lazaro was muttering, as he reached the foot of a short set of metal steps, stretched a leg across a half metre divide of agitated water and entered the hatch. 'I don't want to get involved with any of this again. You and Edwina can do what you like up in Scotland, if these aliens come back for more—but I've had enough. You'll have to find another pathologist to rope in. I don't care *how* much money is on offer. It's too dangerous. I'm not doing the teleport leap to that cave, either. You can go with them and see them through the corridor; collect the payment. I'm getting out of here back the way we came in. In five minutes. I'll need to get well away from this godforsaken place before the reservoir wall blows. Or those crazy fish smash their way in.'

Spin heard all of this while he put down the red case, took off the white lab coat, clambered into the hatch and, reaching back, tied one of the sleeves tightly around the lowest metal step on the platform. Then he attached the hem to the edge of the red flashing circle he was standing in, with a bulldog clip from one of his pockets. He gave a little wave of encouragement to the blackness and then went down the rungs.

It was in the short corridor at the foot of the hatch that Lazaro finally worked out that he'd let in an interloper. Spin stood quietly behind him as he opened a door with the gentle turn of a silver wheel. The door clicked but only moved slightly inward. 'Watch out for them,' Lazaro said. 'They're weak but they're crafty. That bird of theirs attacked me. Edwina's going to have to get them in the wiping chamber. They won't go easily.'

Then he turned around, saw Spin, and made a croaking noise of shock and bewilderment. Spin had his arms out wide, black fingernails grazing the walls on either side; red lining on show and his fangs out. He'd seen many an expression like this, on countless dark nights around Thornleigh. He'd always got a huge kick out of scaring people—but nothing like this. This was better than all the rest. He was ramped up on adrenalin, and sharp . . . very sharp. And the blackness was travelling with him, to complete the effect.

Before Lazaro could utter a word he was pinned to the floor, scrabbling on his back like a tipped-over beetle, helpless and hopeless. Spin held him still and dropped his fangs to the man's trembling throat out of pure habit. Then he pulled back, remembering he had other stuff to do. 'You know what?' he said. 'You'll keep.' Then, in one swift and brutal move, he rendered the man senseless.

He stood and pushed open the door. He stepped up over its high threshold and then paused to yank Lazaro's arm across it for a doorstop.

The blackness was following him. He took comfort from the company. 'Ladies,' he said. 'Follow me.'

CHAPTER 42

'On the stools please,' said Edwina. 'And then hold on to the handles on either side. Don't struggle or resist. Relax. It's much easier if you do. In a couple of minutes you'll be perfectly happy. Then we'll transport you.'

'Where to?' asked Tima, scrubbing the tears off her face. 'Where does that thing take us to? Please . . . just . . . explain what will happen.'

Edwina sighed as she fiddled around with a panel of lights and buttons on a console facing the cubicles, still brandishing the Taser in one hand. 'It's a short-range teleporter. You know— like in Star Trek, only real. But it can't beam you all the way to the new planet; the technology is light-years beyond any Earth tech, but it still only works within a three kilometre radius. You'll be teleported across the town and into the cave where the corridor comes through.'

'Corridor,' repeated Elena, glancing at them both. They knew about the corridor, even if they'd never found the cave. A shame, thought Tima, that by the time they finally got to see exactly where their nightly beam came in and out, they wouldn't have any memory of what it meant.

'Yes,' said Edwina, sounding distracted as the machine she was wrangling began to hum. 'It's a kind of wormhole to other planets. There are two corridor key points in the UK, both in undiscovered caves. One in Scotland and one down here in little old Thornleigh. I've sent pets through from both. Now shut up, please. Let's get this done. We're down to eight minutes before this whole damn thing gets vaporized and I think we'd all like to be safely over in the cave by then.'

She waved the Taser from Tima to Matt to Elena. 'I'm not joking about using this,' she said. 'Get on the stools and hold the handles if you want to live.'

The stools were made of some kind of plastic but the handles, set into either side of the cubicles, were metal. Tima sat on her stool and then paused, wondering what to do. Was having your mind wiped and being sent to an alien planet any better than getting hit by a Taser and staying here to be vaporized? She couldn't make herself grasp the handles.

Above them, a long metal gantry was lowering from the ceiling. White light was chasing backwards and forwards along it in tiny beads. The gantry lowered to just above their heads.

The gantry was humming, revving up, its pitch rising.

'Look at the light,' said Edwina. 'And hold the handles.'

Still Tima could not make herself obey. She was not going. She *couldn't* do it. There was a tingling in her skin . . . some kind of dumb hope that they could all be saved. That if she just waited a few seconds more . . .

There was a green flash. The holographic figure arrived above the console. 'What is the delay?' it demanded. 'You have six minutes.'

'I know, I *know*,' said Edwina, tetchily. 'I'm *managing* this undesirable situation. *You're* the one who set up the countdown. Would it have hurt just to wait until everyone was transported and then blow this thing?'

'It is *you* who is at fault,' the alien said. '*You* recruited Castle and Lazaro. You chose badly. They revealed their plans in full hearing of these other children. They allowed themselves to be tracked. *I* am only clearing up the mess you have made. Maybe I should not bother and let you all be tracked down by the authorities.'

'And lose your only suppliers?' grunted Edwina. 'I don't think—WHAT THE HELL IS THAT?' There was panic in her voice.

Tima jumped off the stool and crouched down, staring across the floor. On either side of her Matt and Elena did the same. A tide of blackness was sweeping in through the door to the dome room. At first it just looked like smoke, bubbling and drifting, but the tingle across her skin told Tima it was much more than this. The smell of vinegar was overwhelming.

'GET BACK ON THOSE STOOLS!' yelled Edwina. Then, to the alien: 'It's all right . . . It's just some smoke . . . and

'. . . ants.'

'Do NOT bring any insects through.' The alien sounded panicked.

The red lights began to flash at double speed and now a shrill horn began tooting.

'Five minutes!' yelled Edwina. 'We have to GO! You three have got thirty seconds to decide to live or die!'

Tima made the decision. She shot across the floor and pulled open the door. The first thing she saw was Spin, barrelling towards her in a cloud of smoke. She ducked sideways to let him pass. The next thing she saw was the ants. All over the inside of the dome, spraying formic acid against the glass. She could barely see past them to the outside where the lake animals were now in a frenzy, hurling themselves at the barrier.

Behind her she could hear Edwina screaming 'GET THEM OFF ME!'

The red lights flashed even faster and the warning horn rose a pitch higher and the whole structure gave a deep, strained groan. *Three minutes*, she guessed. *Maybe two.* She closed her eyes, sent a *thank you* to the ants, sent a *goodbye* to her poor mum and dad.

And got ready either to drown or be vaporized.

CHAPTER 43

Spin had heard voices on the far side of the door which stood
ajar in the white wall, just before he set off his smoke bombs. He
knew the Night Speakers were there and guessed that whatever
he, the ants, and the fish had in mind, there was very little time
to make it count. Over the years he had learnt that surprise was
one of his best assets. There was no time to creep. He detonated
his black smoke effect and shoved open the door. A deluge of
ants rushed in with him, probably seeking out their mistress,
Tima.

And there she was, cannoning out towards him. He
sidestepped her and she sidestepped him, her face blanched
with a mixture of fear and wonder. She was heading in the right
direction—back to the hatch corridor. But what about Elena?
He bashed the door wide open and saw four kids in matching

grey shorts and T-shirts sitting motionless under glowing green columns of light. They stared blankly at him as a mousy-looking woman waved a Taser gun around, yelling at a holographic figure floating in the air: 'You'll have to teleport us NOW! Leave the others here!' Meanwhile Elena and Matt were on their knees, staring at up him, mouths agape.

He lost no time. He threw out one flat hand and struck the Taser out of the woman's grasp with a crack. He expected her to topple over with the impact but in fact she came right back at him with some well-practised karate strikes and kicks. 'GO!' yelled Spin towards Elena, ducking under a punch. 'The hatch is open. GO!'

Elena sprinted past Spin, Matt hot on her heels, and back into the dome which was now darkly seething with millions . . . maybe *billions* . . . of ants. There were so many ravaging the glass they were even hanging down in stalactite formation in places. Tima stood in the middle of the chamber staring around her. 'It's going,' she said, her face waxy and peculiarly still in the relentless flashing red. 'They're attacking the glass and all the seals with formic acid. It's dissolving. It will collapse. There won't be a big explosion.'

'Come ON!' yelled Elena. 'The door is open! We have to GO!' She grabbed her friend's arm and hauled her towards the open door leading to the corridor and the hatch, just as there was a groan and a crack. Matt gave a shout as a gush of water began to jet into the chamber at pressure-hose force.'

'WAIT! The others!' yelled Matt. Elena and Tima turned,

staring across a growing waterfall at their friend. 'You go on!' he called above the tooting alarm. 'I'm just going to see—'

Then the groaning, cracking dome gave further and the waterfall doubled in width, bringing fish and eels with it, writhing across the silver floor.

Elena couldn't even see Matt now. A spear of horror shot through her to think of losing him, but she took in a sharp breath, grabbed Tima and dragged her towards the corridor which was now calf-deep in water.

Any other time Spin would have loved it. The woman was clearly black belt level and her moves were excellent for someone at least twenty years his senior. But the flashing red light and the dumb kids and the sense that everything was going to blow in a matter of seconds . . . it was a bit distracting. Now a deep bass hum began to build up on the platform.

As he glanced across at it, the woman got the better of him and he found himself swiped off his feet and lying on his back on the floor beside a plastic stool. He was vaguely aware of Matt back in the room, shouting at the dopey kids in the PE kits. And through the open oval door he could see an alarming amount of gushing water and at least three jagged-toothed fish flipping around in it.

The woman was hopping up onto platform alongside the vacant kids. 'NOW!' she was bawling. 'NOW!'

Spin thought it might be a good time to get out of here. Elena and Tima should have escaped by now and Matt could *probably* take care of himself. The lake was making its surprise entrance through the roof; that horn was pounding through his skull and the flashing red light wasn't telling him to relax and wait for his flight, either. Set into the cubicle around the stool was a pair of metal rungs. Spin grasped them, pulling himself up, glanced up at a line of blinking white lights on a metal strut just above him . . .

. . . and forgot everything.

CHAPTER 44

Lazaro nearly cost them their lives. He was lying, unconscious, on the rapidly-flooding floor of the corridor as Elena dragged Tima along it. They fell over him.

'He'll drown if we leave him here,' Elena gasped.

'Let him,' said Tima. 'He was ready to drown our town.'

But Elena was already dragging the man upright. His eyes flickered open and then widened in alarm at the raucous shriek of the countdown. 'Come ON!' Elena yelled at him, dropping Tima's arm to grab his. 'We've got SECONDS left!'

At last he got to his feet and began to wade through the water after them.

They made it to the ladder and began to climb, fear driving them fast. Tima reached the surface and found it churning in agitation all around the little brick watershed, throwing the red warning lights around the hatch in all directions. Tima leapt across to the platform and held out her hand for Elena as she emerged.

'Come on, come *on*!' she begged, because every Night Speaker message she was getting was telling her to RUN.

Elena's face told her she was getting the same rolling bulletin.

'It's cracking,' she said. 'But it's going to blow too.'

They heard the Italian scrambling up the ladder inside the hatch but did not stop to wait for him. They tore back up the concrete steps to the door of the monitoring station. For a moment Tima feared it might be solidly shut against their escape, but no, brambles were pulled into the frame, keeping it ajar. A few lines of ants were still climbing through it and heading towards the stairs and the hatch. 'No!' Tima puffed. 'Don't go down there. You've done enough. Thank you.'

They ran through the thorny weeds, their bare feet and legs getting grazed and sliced by the rough terrain.

'This way!' Elena said, pulling Tima round to the other side of the hut and on towards the top end of the reservoir. 'Don't stop!'

The kids on the platform stared at Matt like cattle as he bellowed at them to move.

'LEAVE THEM ALONE!' screamed Edwina as she scrambled into a column of green light.

Matt ran for Liam and one of the girls, grabbing their arms and bellowing at them to move. Amazingly, they got to their feet.

'THREE,' called the alien hologram, flickering and breaking up above the console.

'LEAVE THEM!' screamed Edwina, trying to grab hold of Megan.

Matt dragged Liam and Kacey along towards the door, nearly tripping over Spin's outstretched legs.

'TWO!' called the hologram.

The other two kids, watching their fellow pets move, followed, stepping down from the platform and walking slowly across the rapidly-flooding floor.

'WA—'

There was a flash of green light and then the woman and the hologram were gone. Matt shoved the empty kids towards the door and turned back to see Spin getting to his feet and staring around, looking blank.

'This way!' Matt bellowed. But there wasn't really any way. Water was pouring through the door and rising rapidly. It was already up to their waists. Five seconds later it was at his chest and his feet were lifting off the floor. The others bobbed around him, looking vaguely concerned. It was shockingly cold. He hoped Elena and Tima had made it out in time, but for him, there was no escape now. Not for him or the wiped, empty kids. He glanced back at the glassy face of the vampire boy who had filled him with such intense anger and loathing . . . maybe even more than Liam had . . . for so many months now. What a way to end; drowning in the company of his two worst enemies.

The red light flashed so fast now it was just a flicker. The tooting stopped and for two or three seconds, before he went under, it seemed almost peaceful.

CHAPTER 45

Tima pelted after Elena, along a winding, overgrown path which reached gently upwards. Her feet and legs stung, and her lungs felt like they might burst beyond her ribcage. The sky was just beginning to get light in the east and a chink of moonlight, through a break in the clouds, shone across the flat pale stretch of wall that held this massive body of water in place, high above Thornleigh.

Below them, there was a rumble and a tangible thickness in the air. Tima glanced back to see the top of the lake *shaking* . . . myriad bubbles were coming to the surface. Perfectly round marbles of water were shooting up and then landing back down again in a mass of spreading concentric circles. 'I think it's going to blow!' Elena yelled. 'It's still going to blow! We have to get higher!'

They sprinted for the reservoir wall, finding a nanosecond of relief as their wounded feet hit the smooth, flat concrete path that led up onto the embankment. As the tree cover was left behind they had a perfect view on either side. To Tima's left was their town, nestling in its valley, lights twinkling up, peaceful and completely oblivious to the terrifying danger it was in. To her right was the reservoir, boiling and shaking. Fish and all kinds of other aquatic souls were leaping out of the water and arcing through the air, trying to escape. A white cloud at the far end seemed to lift off and hover in the darkness.

The shadowy outline of a man could be made out, running back towards the car park area; Lazaro had got that far at least. It might not be enough, thought Tima. She and Elena came to a halt. There were at the dead-centre of the embankment now. There was no higher place they could reach. They wrapped their arms around each other, pressing their shoulders back up against the wall and bracing against what every animal in the area was now signalling to them. Time up.

The boom, when it came, was not so much a noise as a shock wave. A perfect circle suddenly appeared, dipping down like a shallow bowl. Then it inverted and shot upwards—a mass of water shaped like a mushroom—high, high into the air. For a moment it seemed to hang there, suspended and weirdly beautiful in the moonlight.

But gravity won. As Tima watched it drop, she knew the tsunami that followed would be terrifying.

CHAPTER 46

It was a ballet. Almost beautiful. Spin didn't know why he was here and he suspected it was probably not a good place to be, but all around him were bubbles and shining scales and people whose hair floated like water weed across their smooth, smooth faces.

He held his breath. One thing he *did* know was that inhaling water was a bad thing. So he just didn't. He looked around instead. The red insides of his coat rippled past his eyes. A silvery snake-like thing stroked his cheek.

Matt felt the force of the explosion . . . or was it an implosion? It shook every organ in his body. He managed not to suck in a breath, even so. Nearby, Liam Bassiter was floating, his eyes wide and surprised, as if someone had just ducked him at the swimming pool. Bubbles streamed out of his nose.

Some powerful vortex spun Matt around. He saw the others move into its curve; Spin's stupid vampire coat flapping out behind him as if he was really flying like a bat.

Matt tried to pull some better last thoughts into his mind. Then he was somewhat distracted by being flung several metres into the air.

The next thing Spin knew, he was looking at the moon. It seemed very familiar. But the drag of his wet clothes against his body as he flew upwards was something entirely new. For a moment he got a widescreen view of this scene. He was in a cloud of water droplets, fish, people, otters, eels; every creature was striking an unlikely pose; limbs, heads, wings, claws, fins, spinning out inelegantly in all directions.

Then, a moment later, they all got organized and headed in the same direction. Down.

What air had been left in his lungs was instantly expelled as Matt struck the surface of the lake. He crashed through it and on down to its bed, ears roaring, grazing his feet and knees on some jagged outcrop. Then he was rising up again, helpless to do anything but go with the force of the water. He couldn't even see the others now. His vision was gone. His lungs were squeezed flat inside him. Soon he would open his mouth and drag in the water; he couldn't stop that compulsion. Soon. But not . . . quite . . . yet . . .

It was taking him a horribly long time to die.
Something bit his arm.

CHAPTER 47

The tsunami was a perfect circle. It rose up like a slick, wet bowl on a potter's wheel and spread across the lake in every direction. As it moved it rose higher and higher.

Elena felt fluttering in her chest. No ... she felt fluttering *against* her chest. Glancing down she saw Lucky was with her, trying to catch a hold of her soaked T-shirt and hide in her hair. She had no time to tell the bird to fly. The water was rising towards them. The smooth curve began to wobble and froth as it came into contact with the closer shores and inlets; trees were waving wildly and some were toppling.

Hadn't they helped at all, Tima's ants? So many of them, dissolving the glass and the seals, breaking the structure, taking away the impact before the countdown ended ... was it all for nothing?

The water smashed into the monitoring station and rolled on up towards them. A white cloud descended across Elena's eyes and she felt Lucky tremble against her throat. A peculiar coolness struck her; perhaps this is what people felt when they could see their end coming.

But actually, no, it was more than a coolness. It was a rush of cold air. Elena and Tima stared up in amazement. Above them were swans and geese, flapping their wings at amazing speed. The downdraught was like something from a helicopter. Elena shrank down, clinging to Tima as the water came up and up and up . . .

. . .and then slowed. Rising still . . . but not so fast. The energy in it was dwindling. The downdraught was making it pucker and prickle, pushing it back. The noise of the wings . . . hundreds of wings . . . was tremendous. Elena scooped Lucky tighter into her, scared she might be blown away.

Then the flock rose and scattered and they were left, crouched on the concrete, staring at the receding wave while behind them the town of Thornleigh slept on, untroubled.

CHAPTER 48

Being saved by otters is not a gentle thing. Matt realized this as he was tugged through the dying tsunami by three powerful, furry swimmers. Each was hanging onto him by their teeth, one at each shoulder and one on his left hip. They were trying to be gentle and only nip into the material of his flimsy grey outfit, but his skin would bear the scars. Not that he had any strength left to complain. Or to help them. He lay, face upwards, drawing in stuttering gasps of air whenever he could, watching a cloud of white birds scattering into the sky while his rescuers swam powerfully for the shore, dragging him across the choppy, churning water.

Something was underneath his back, giving him a boost. It was smooth, about the length of him, and incredibly strong. It was only as he was pulled up to the shore and it flipped up a

tapering silvery tail and sank away that he realized it was
an eel.

The otters pulled him up on a soggy patch of vegetation
which had once been dry land . . . before the underwater dome
had imploded or exploded or whatever it had done. He lay,
his head in a pillow of tufty, soggy grass, and wondered if he
would ever be able to move or speak again. Had they saved
Thornleigh? Was the reservoir even now emptying a killer
flood onto the people below?

He became aware of more struggling through the water
and realized his otter rescue squad was now dragging another
body up onto the shore. It had the same clothing on as
him, so it must be one of the other pets. He rolled over and
threw up some water, gasping and choking until he faded
out of consciousness. When he came to, he was shivering
uncontrollably. It wasn't from fear—he was way past anything
like that. It was the cold. He was lying outside on a November
night, wearing next to nothing and soaking wet. It was a
miracle he was still alive . . . but he might not be for much
longer. Exposure was probably going to kill him before dawn.

Matt felt something furry press against his arm. Not wet
fur this time; dry. He turned his head and stared straight into
the concerned dark eyes of Velma. She hadn't come alone.
She was accompanied by three of her cubs—nearly fully-
grown foxes now. She made a low grunting noise and they all
clustered around him, pressing their warm fur against his cold,
clammy skin. It felt wonderful.

Dotted along the banks were others, too. Foxes, badgers,

and even some young deer, were all gathered around the human flotsam that had been laid out to dry.

Picking her way along the storm-ravaged shore of the reservoir, Elena found two bodies beneath the mammals. Kacey and Lewis. They were conscious. Shocked and pale and unspeaking, but conscious. They stared up at her with wide, wide eyes and when she gave them something which passed for a smile, although she was shocked and crying, they smiled back vacantly.

Tima shouted that she'd found Liam, too. Also awake. Also quiet and smiling back. Of Megan there was no trace.

And there was no sign of Spin. Or Matt.

'Here!' Tima shouted. 'He's here!'

Elena didn't know who she meant. Matt? Or Spin? She ran towards the foxes and Velma sent her a pulse of relieved welcome.

'Matt! Talk to me!' Tima was saying, slapping him gently on the cheeks.

Elena leaned over as the foxes made space for them. 'Sit him up,' she said. 'We've got to get him somewhere warm and dry.' She glanced around, dismayed. 'We've got to get them all somewhere warm and dry. But I don't know how.'

'They're being kept warm,' said Tima. 'Don't worry. We can call for help for them. But first . . . Matt.'

They hauled him up into a sitting position and Elena put her hands on his face and stared into his eyes. 'Matt! Matt— say something.' Matt just stared at her. There was blood on his shoulders. She forced herself to smile at him, heart thudding, dreading his reaction. Matt did not smile back. He didn't do anything. Then there was a flurry of dark feathers and Lucky landed on his head. Matt blinked, gave a huge shudder, coughed, and said: 'Let's go home.'

They helped him back to the car park and found that only the Ford was there. The black BMW was gone. Inside the car they sat for a while, as the engine idled and warmth began to flood through the air conditioning grilles. It was flukily good luck that Matt had forgotten to lock the car when they'd arrived, earlier. He had just switched off the engine and left the key in the ignition. Had he kept the key in his jeans pocket, it would be somewhere out in the reservoir now.

'Do you think you can drive?' Elena asked him, as he sat in the driver seat, slowly getting a little less numb. He nodded.

'What . . . what should we do? What should we say?' Elena said. 'We've got to get help for Kacey, Liam, and Lewis. And we need to search for Megan . . . and Spin. How . . . how are we *ever* going to explain everything that's happened tonight?'

'We're not,' said Matt. 'We're just going home. We can call 999 and send ambulances up here for the others—and the animals will look after them and keep them warm until the people arrive.'

'But what about Spin?' asked Elena. 'He came in to save us. We have to try to find him.'

Matt nodded slowly. 'We'll do a circuit of the lake; see if we can find him or Megan. And then . . .' he pointed to the clock on the car's dashboard: 4.58 a.m. 'Then we have to go. We have to get to a callbox and get the ambulances . . . then home. Being here when all the blue lights show up will not help anyone.'

They got out of the car reluctantly and, staying close to each other, travelled around the shore, scouring the frothing waves and the debris of broken trees for a sign of Spin or Megan. As they passed each of the other rescued kids, each in their furry living incubators, they checked on them; found them warmer, calm, and still gently smiling. None of them spoke when spoken to, but they seemed to be OK.

'Do you think it will wear off?' whispered Tima, as they picked their way further along the shore, Matt shining the single torch they'd found in the Ford's glove compartment.

'I don't know,' said Matt. 'They've been wiped, haven't they? It sounded pretty permanent when that Italian guy was explaining it. What happened to hi—?' Matt stopped abruptly and pointed ahead. Lying on its side in the shallows, a short distance from the gravel road, was the black BMW. He ran to it, his bare feet slipping and sloshing through the water, and shone in his torch. Lazaro and Castle were both inside. The car windows were open and the detritus from the tsunami was scattered across their semi-submerged bodies. They must have tried to out-drive the water, Matt realized. They'd failed.

He walked back to Elena and Tima, shaking his head. 'Do yourself a favour,' he said. 'Take my word for it; they're both dead.'

They never found Megan. Elena knew Tima would be haunted by that. She had cared about that poor girl. Even as they headed back to the car, exhausted and silent, the message was coming through from the animals. Megan had not made it. She was still in the reservoir.

Elena closed her eyes, scared to ask. But she had to. *Spin . . . ?*

There was a long pause . . . and then a pulse of information, carried in on the electric atmosphere which crackled between them and the animal world these days. She let out a long sigh. Spin was not dead. Where was he?

'Spin's on the boat,' said Tima, clearly on the same wildlife wavelength. She turned and pointed out a light glowing dimly at the end of the reservoir where the canal came in. It was moving away from them and soon disappeared in the trees. 'He's fine,' added Tima. 'Or . . . you know . . . as fine as the rest of us, which is . . .'

' . . . not very fine,' said Matt. 'Come on. We need to call for help for the others.'

He drove them slowly back along the gravelly road and down into the town. It was nearly 6 a.m. and the sky in the east was significantly lighter as Elena hopped out at the call box on the edge of the town centre, tucked away in the shadow of a tall bank building. Happily, it wasn't vandalized and she dialled 999.

'There's been an explosion and a big flood up at Thornleigh reservoir. There are several children who need help. And . . . two dead guys in a car,' she told the operator. 'Get ambulances up there as soon as you can. This isn't a hoax.' Then she slammed down the receiver, cutting off the demands to know who and where she was.

Matt dropped Tima off first. They watched her creep around the back of the house. She had no key, of course; that was deep underwater along with her clothes and her mobile phone. But she said she knew how to get in through a downstairs window. They waited for five minutes until they saw her face emerge around her bedroom curtains, then they waved and drove on.

Lucky perched on Matt's shoulder, staying close, as he turned the car in along Elena's road. 'Can you get in?' he said.

She nodded. 'There's a spare key hidden under a pot in the front garden. Mum's terrible for locking herself out. Listen . . .'

They could hear distant sirens and see blue lights winding up the hillside roads towards the reservoir. What would the paramedics make of the clusters of mammals keeping their patients warm? Maybe the animals would flee before they were seen.

'I've got to go,' said Matt. 'Dad'll be up soon.'

'Can *you* get in?' asked Elena.

'Yeah. Spare key in the tyre shed. I'm good.'

'Are you sure?' Elena peered at him, resting her fingers on the car door handle. 'You haven't even told me what happened down there? In the dome?'

'It'll keep,' said Matt, shrugging. He glanced in the rear-view mirror.

'What the hell are we going to tell them about our hair?'

CHAPTER 49

Spin wasn't sure how he got from under the water to up on
the boat. He was dimly aware of something pulling him up
to the surface, battling hard against the fierce push and pull
of the waves. Something had dragged him across the lake and
deposited him beneath the low branch where this boat was tied
up. It had taken him a while to get up onto the bank, his coat
saturated and heavy, and he was sick twice. Then he got on the
boat. It looked easy to drive. It needed a key. He felt around in
his many wringing wet pockets and found a bunch of keys. One
of them fitted the ignition panel on the boat. Its engine started
up without much noise. He spent a few minutes working out the
basics, how to steer, how to move forward; how to reverse . . . it
was pretty simple. Then he steered the boat away from the bank,
across the choppy lake and towards the canal.

As the vessel moved along the dark channel of water, its single headlamp cutting a slice of light through the gloom, a white owl swooped low over his head and flew back the way he'd come. He thought he had maybe done this before. And when he reached the tall brick arch spanning the canal, he instinctively slowed and brought the boat to the bank.

Something had happened? What had happened? He felt a deep and empty silence inside himself. It was . . . a bit like . . . when you woke from someone screaming at you in a dream, to find yourself in a completely quiet room . . . the echo of the dream scream still reverberating through your mind but the actual silence boxing your ears.

What was the scream about? Why was he wet? Why did the inside of his leg hurt? Why was he so very, very tired?

He killed the engine, pocketed the key and tied up the boat to metal rings in the wooden edge of the bank where he thought he'd maybe tied it up before. Then he paused; looked around; made his way towards a wood. Time was slipping, like his wet socks inside his boots. *Slip*. Now he was deep in the wood. *Slip*. Now he was at a high brick wall and a wrought-iron gate. *Slip*. Now walking down the steps to a room.

He switched on a light. It was a dim light, heavily shaded, but it picked out his tall, thin, dark form in a wall-to-floor mirror.

He walked up to it, staring. The face that looked back at him was pale and bruised. He put out a hand and touched his strange reflection.

'Who the hell . . .' he asked, ' . . . are you?'

CHAPTER 50

Tima had less than an hour in her bed before it was time to get up for school. Her SpongeBob alarm clock went off at seven. She hadn't slept. She'd simply curled up under her quilt and tried to stop shivering. She was going to have to say she was ill; there was no way she could get through school.

Mum came in ten minutes later, to chivvy her out of bed.

'Nooo, Mum. Don't open the curtains,' mumbled Tima. 'My head hurts.'

Mum sat on the edge of her bed and felt her forehead. 'You don't feel hot,' she said. 'If anything you're a bit cold and clammy.'

'I think I need to stay in bed,' said Tima, and her voice croaked helpfully. 'No—no light!' She swiped Mum's hand away from the bedside lamp switch.

'Tima, if you can't stand the light, it could be something serious,' said Mum, looking concerned.

'I know . . . meningitis,' said Tima. You didn't have to be the daughter of a surgeon to know the symptoms of brain inflammation. 'It's not that bad. I just . . . didn't sleep well.'

Mum sighed. 'I really thought you'd got past that,' she said.

'I have,' said Tima, quickly. 'I mean, most of the time. Last night was just . . . a funny night.'

Mum got up. 'Sleep on for a bit, then,' she said. 'I'll check in on you. Luckily I haven't got any visits to make today. You'll probably feel better by lunchtime.'

Tima burrowed under the quilt and slept. Mum did check in an hour later and Tima woke, but kept her eyes shut. As soon as Mum had gone downstairs she got up and crept to the bathroom. In the mirror her hair was clumped and messy . . . and dark red.

She grabbed a bottle of shampoo, stepped into the shower, and hoped for the best.

The deaths up at the reservoir and the strange appearance of three unidentified teenagers were all over the radio news as Matt soaped the Ford. He worked at great speed and got it done, moving on to a Toyota just as Dad came down. Then he got a cuff around the back of the head for being lazy and only just starting. Because the Ford, of course, had been cleaned *yesterday*—until Matt and his friends had seriously dirtied it up again in the night. There had been no hope of any sleep for Matt.

The grey woollen hat he was wearing took the sting out of

his father's blow. And because it was a cold November morning, Dad didn't question the headgear. Matt reckoned he'd have half an hour to get in the shower and shampoo the colour out if he cleaned the Toyota at top speed.

He almost collapsed in the shower. He'd had less than two hours sleep in the last twenty-four. He was running on empty. But the red dye, at least, washed out of his hair in soapy ginger rivulets across the white shower tray. If it had been permanent, he had no idea how he would have explained it.

As he staggered out in his dressing gown, Mum took one look at him and said: 'You are ill!'

Matt nodded, groggily. 'I think I might have flu,' he croaked. His unstoppable shivering helped to sell that idea. Mum sent him straight to bed, ignoring his father's protests that he was putting it on.

'*Look* at him!' he heard Mum say. Dad looked and grunted and let Matt be.

'Nice hair colour,' said Mum.

Elena blinked awake and saw a small plate of digestive biscuits and a mug of tea steaming gently on the bedside table next to the clock. The clock said 10.10 a.m. Elena sat up. 'I should be in school!' she said. 'Why didn't you wake me?'

'Didn't wake up myself until half an hour ago,' said Mum, sitting on her bed and sipping from her own mug. She was in her dressing gown. 'And you looked like you could use a morning off. I already called them and said you were ill.'

Elena sank back onto her pillow. She wanted to cry. Wanted

to bury her head against Mum's shoulder and tell her everything. Instead, she took a deep breath and let it out again, slowly. 'The hair thing is just a temporary colour. Got a free sample. Thought it might look nice.'

'You look beautiful in any hair colour,' said Mum, stroking a strand back from her daughter's forehead. 'Could use some conditioner, though. It feels a bit gritty.' She patted around Elena's head. 'Flippineck! Have you been mud diving?!'

'Yeah,' said Elena. 'Went out last night and dragged my head through a pond.'

'I used to put henna on my hair when I was your age,' Mum went on. 'It was like a big bowl of cowpat!'

Elena smiled and then felt the smile wobble and tears began to roll down her face.

'Oh sweetheart, what is it? What's wrong?' Mum leaned in and hugged her. 'It's not the hair, is it? You look lovely, I told you!'

Elena sniffed, laughing a little at the ludicrous thought that she'd cry over a little hair dye. With all the things she *really* had to cry about after last night. 'No,' she said. 'It's nothing. I just . . . it's . . . there's this . . .'

' . . . boy?' Mum filled in, one eyebrow raised.

Elena paused and then nodded. Why not? A boy *was* part of it. She was really afraid of what had happened to Spin. The message they'd all got was that he was alive. The message was *not* that he was OK.

'Is it that Spin character?' asked Mum, looking knowing . . . while knowing nothing.

Elena nodded again. 'I've just been a bit . . . worried about him.'

'Are you two . . . you know . . . ?'

'No. No, not that,' Elena said. 'I'm not sure *what* we are, really. I'm not even sure he's a friend. He messes with my mind, that's all.'

'So what are you worried about?' asked Mum.

Elena drew a blank. What could she say? 'I don't know,' she murmured, reaching for her mug of tea. 'I think I'm just tired. Tired and emotional.'

'Well, have some tea and eat some biscuits . . . and go back to sleep,' said Mum.

And at that point, Elena could think of no better remedy.

CHAPTER 51

The news was full of the deaths of two prominent consultants from Thornleigh hospital and the discovery of three teenagers who had been *thought* to be dead ... and a fourth who was dead but had been thought deceased and buried days before.

The national press was all over it too. As it slowly emerged, across the next few days, who the teenagers were, the story got only more astonishing. Neither the two boys nor the girl appeared to remember anything. They were all calm and agreeable and gave no signs that they'd been through any trauma ... although they clearly had. It was soon uncovered that there was nothing but bags of flour in the coffins where each had apparently been laid to rest in recent weeks—and that the dead paediatrician and pathologist had both been involved in their hospital care and in falsifying their deaths. The funeral director handling the burials had been arrested for questioning. A social worker who was linked to them all was being sought by police.

'Thornleigh Hospital and social services are undertaking a wide-ranging enquiry into this unprecedented series of events,' said a reporter on the lunchtime news. 'At this point there is much speculation as to the reason why these children were certified dead when they were still alive. The three survivors— and the dead girl who was later discovered in Thornleigh reservoir on Monday—were all wearing the same clothes and seem to have been kept in the same place; an underwater observatory built in the 1960s and left derelict since the 1980s. It's thought they may have been abducted and held for trafficking—or even for the sale of organs.'

'This town is getting weirder and weirder,' said Astrid, from the other end of the sofa.

'Certainly is,' said Spin, smiling.

'Helps *you* to fit in, anyway.' Astrid leaned over and mussed his hair. 'How are you feeling?'

'I'm fine,' said Spin.

'Are you?' She stared at him from her gloomy side of the room. A shaft of sunlight lay across his face so he couldn't see her expression too well—but he knew what it would be. Worried. This was his mother. He called her Astrid. And she was worried.

What else? Ah yes. She had a blood disorder which meant she could not tolerate light; not sun or cloud or even bright lamps indoors. He had the disorder too but he'd recently been treated in hospital for it and so he was able, for the first time in many years, to sit here with the sun on his face without whimpering in agony.

She was worried because he was not himself. He knew this was true. He was definitely not himself. He wasn't sure whether this was a good or a bad thing, because whenever he got flashes of memory about the Spin who *had been* himself, before whatever had happened had happened, it didn't look too wholesome. Out at night. Creeping around in the dark. Fighting. Biting.

Or maybe he'd just been watching some cheesy TV series about vampires and was somehow having false memory syndrome.

'I'm not sure it was worth it,' Astrid said, suddenly, muting the TV and sitting up to look at him more closely. 'The blood exchange. It's only a short-term fix anyway and it's taken so much out of you. That's why I held off for so long. Why I didn't want them to mess with you.'

'But it's worked,' said Spin. He smiled again and she looked ill at ease. He was smiling too much, apparently. 'I can go outside. It doesn't hurt any more.'

She nodded. 'Yes. Yes, it does seem to have helped you.' She glanced out of the window. 'But it seems to have knocked out some of your . . . energy. Your . . . fight.'

'I can still fight you,' said Spin. It was true. She'd attacked him twice since he'd got back in the house on the night of the time slips and he'd instinctively defended himself with well-oiled martial arts moves on both occasions.

'That's not really what I mean,' she said. She sighed,

looking out of the window again. 'I think we should go out this afternoon. Take a gentle walk through the park.'

'What about you?' Spin asked. 'You haven't been treated. You'll be in pain.'

'Not if I cover up,' said Astrid. 'And it's winter sun, anyway. Not as bad as summer sun. I'll put on my hat and gloves and glasses. It'll be fine. I want to see you enjoying the daytime for a change. We can buy hot dogs if you like.'

'OK,' said Spin. 'Let's do that.' He smiled at her again. He was very fond of her. She was his mother.

She smiled back, a little sadly. He hoped he could get back the energy and the fight she wanted. He wasn't sure how to do it. Maybe he would run a bit; punch the air like a boxer working out. That might make her happy.

'Come on,' she said, getting up.

He got up and followed her. She turned around in the hallway, found him close behind her, and looked startled. Then she took a deep breath and said: 'You can go to your room and get your shoes and coat on.'

'OK,' he said.

And so that's what he did.

CHAPTER 52

'Everyone's talking about it,' said Matt, falling into step with Elena as they left school. It was Friday afternoon. They'd both been back in school since Tuesday and still, nothing seemed normal. Elena kept getting sudden palpitations; surges of adrenalin, stabs of fear.

'I know,' she muttered. 'I can't get away from it.'

'They say Liam's going to a new family,' said Matt. 'After they showed them all on telly, there were floods of calls from families offering to adopt. It's like one of those TV shows at Battersea Dogs' Home.'

Elena nodded. 'Yep.' She'd seen the news video of the three kids who'd come back from the dead. They all looked pale, calm, and incredibly sweet. They'd been dressed in nice clothes; had their hair washed and brushed. Their health check-ups had, bafflingly, pronounced them fit and well with no sign of the heart disorders which had been diagnosed by Castle. 'Do you think . . .' she began, and then stopped because it seemed an awful thing to think, let alone say out loud.

'What?' asked Matt, signalling to Lucky, who was perched on a street lamp further down the road.

'Nothing,' said Elena.

'I know what you're thinking,' said Matt, catching Lucky on his fist and helping her onto his shoulder. 'You're thinking Liam and the others are probably happier now than they used to be. That getting "wiped" has been good for them.'

'Is that a terrible thing to think?' Elena peered across at him.

'No. It's probably true,' Matt said. 'It's not like they had many happy memories to hang on to, is it? They'd all had rough starts. Liam's parents were drug addicts—did you know that? They were dead by the time he was three. Then he was with his nan . . . and then with foster families when she couldn't cope. Ahmed told me.'

'You're speaking to Ahmed again?' she asked.

'Yeah. Now and again. Not in Punjabi, though. I'm hoping he'll forget that.'

'Hmmm,' said Elena. 'Not likely.' She sighed. 'I guess we won't see Liam back in school again any time soon. Maybe never. Do you think they would have been happy on the new planet . . . if we'd just let them go?'

'We'll never know.' Matt shrugged. 'But they wouldn't have lived very long. And imagine the eggy stink of all that sulphur!'

He was trying to be upbeat and make her laugh, and she

appreciated it, but she didn't have much humour in her right now. 'Are you OK?' she asked him. There were cuts and bruises on his body, she knew, but he hadn't let her see.

'I think I'm still in shock, a bit, like you,' he said. 'And I keep worrying the police will trace the tracks of the Ford and find the owner and then find me.'

'Or find all our clothes and phones and stuff in the lake,' said Elena.

Matt shrugged. 'It's nothing we can do anything about. Everything will be washed clean, though. The phones will be dead. We stopped another alien destroying our town. Well—us and the animals. We'll never get thanked because nobody will ever know . . . but that's OK. We just need to take it easy. Get over this. Shall we meet up this weekend? I'm ready to get back to the hide. It still needs more insulation.'

'Yeah,' Elena nodded. 'That would be good. I'm going to meet Tima in the park. I'll tell her. Usual time and place. She's probably got a new phone by now but I haven't. We have to wait for the insurance money to come through.'

'Me too,' said Matt. 'Although I probably shouldn't bother. It'll be my third phone this year. I think me and phones are doomed. See ya.'

And he went off with Lucky on his shoulder, chirping something in his ear. Elena was pleased to see the starling staying close. She knew that Lucky would help Matt get back to some kind of normality.

Tima was waiting for her by the hot dog stand. As Elena approached, her friend waved two hot dogs, wrapped in paper napkins. 'Mum saw you coming and said I could get these for us both. She's just gone to Marks & Spencer. I've got half an hour with you and we can't leave the park!'

'Still grounded then?' Elena asked, taking the roll and hot sausage and catching a bit of dripping ketchup with her tongue.

'Yes,' said Tima. 'It's only because I've been ill that she let me see you today. Hey—your hair still looks a bit red!'

'I know,' said Elena. 'I'm blonder than you and Matt so I think it took a bit more. It fades every time I wash it, though. How did you manage with yours?'

'I washed it out as soon as,' said Tima. 'Mum nearly saw it, but not quite. How's Matt?'

'He's OK,' said Elena. 'Lucky's looking after him. I think—' She broke off, the bread roll halfway to her lips. Across the park, two people were heading across the grass towards the hot dog stand. The woman wore a wide-brimmed black hat, dark glasses, and a scarf wound around her neck. She had gloves on too, and a long trench coat and boots. Her face was out of view, but it wasn't the woman who'd caught Elena's attention. It was the boy walking with her.

He was bouncing along happily, his fair hair flopping across his face, wearing a white sweatshirt and jeans and trainers, oblivious to the chill November air. Every so often he broke into a run and playfully punched out at the air, turning back to watch the woman for a reaction. His movements were puppyish. They made her doubt the evidence of her own eyes. It was only Tima's shocked gasp that made her believe it.

'*SPIN*?!'

Tima looked as astonished as Elena. Her mouth dropped open. 'Or is Spin the evil twin . . . and this guy the nice one?' she whispered, as the pair got closer.

Elena could not stop staring. Spin had always worn black. His hair had always been neatly waxed back off his forehead. The way he moved was sinister and slick. He was pale and interesting; dark and dangerous. A friend one minute, a foe the next. Unpredictable. Unreliable. Anti-hero and hero—all in one night.

And now here was a Spin who looked like the polar opposite of the boy she knew. Yet something about the look on his face, as he drew closer, was horribly familiar.

'Oh god, Tee,' she murmured. 'I know what happened.'

Tima looked up at her, one eyebrow up. 'A gypsy curse was lifted?'

'No . . . he went into that room, didn't he? He came into the dome to find us and he let all the ants in; they got across on the lab coat he tied up for them. Then he came down, saw us, kept the door wedged open . . .'

' . . . with the guy he'd just knocked out . . .' added Tima.

' . . . and then he went on in to find Matt,' said Elena. 'Even though the dome was cracking. And even though Matt hates him. Matt said he came in and started fighting that Edwina woman off while Matt was trying to get the other kids out.'

Tima was silent for a while, watching happy, smiley, daytime Spin collect his hot dog.

'And then . . .' said Elena, and her voice was choked and there was nothing she could do to stop Tima hearing. ' . . . then he must have somehow got wiped. Look at him. Look at his face!'

Spin and the woman with him—his mother, Elena guessed—were walking on with their hot dogs now. Elena and Tima stood, rooted to the ground, as they got closer.

Elena didn't know what to do. Should she call out to him?

But even as she thought this, Spin looked up. His skin was slightly pink and his eyes were still that spectacular turquoise colour, even brighter by day. She locked her own eyes with his and he . . .

. . . looked right through her.

CHAPTER 53

The silver glowing around the walls made Tima a little uneasy. The way their reflections rippled across it when they moved made her remember the underwater dome. It was something she'd really rather forget.

She didn't plan to mention it, though. The hide was coming on so well and was so much warmer. They'd worked hard every night for a week, just until around 4 a.m., so they could get back home to bed and rest properly, even if they weren't sleeping. The night at the reservoir had taken its toll and they all realized they needed some recovery time.

'I know we said we'd stop talking about it for a while,' said Matt, sitting on a beanbag and eating a bag of crisps. 'But— *one*—is it just me or is all that silver a bit freaky?' He glanced around at the rippling reflections in the lamplight.

'I was thinking that,' admitted Elena. 'It makes me think of . . . you know . . .'

Tima sighed with relief. 'I didn't want to say, but, yeah . . .'

'Let's put something else on top of it,' said Elena. 'Some wallpaper or something.'

'Good idea,' said Tima. 'What was number two?' she asked Matt.

'I heard they dragged the reservoir,' said Matt. 'In case they found any more dead kids.'

'Go on,' said Elena, staring warily across her mug.

'They didn't,' said Matt, and Tima and Elena both let out sighs of relief. 'They didn't find much of anything,' he said. 'No alien tech anyway.'

'Well,' said Tima, 'if they *did* find alien tech, do you think they'd tell the press?'

'Good point,' acknowledged Matt. 'They must have seen what the water surge did to the trees and worked out there really was an explosion down there . . . but that hasn't been reported on much. The brain-wiped kids and the plot with the doctors are much more newsworthy, I guess. It's going to run and run, this story.'

'As long as it never runs back to *us*,' muttered Tima.

'Let's let it go, eh?' said Elena, staring into her tomato soup. 'They can figure it out for themselves. We're done.'

Tima wanted to ask her if she was still thinking about Spin, but she bit her lip. She knew Elena wasn't happy that she'd told it all to Matt. Even though Matt had every right to know what had happened in the park. Elena hadn't complained but she was quiet about Spin. She just didn't want to discuss it.

'OK,' said Matt. 'I just wanted you both to know, so we can stop worrying about any police coming for us. I think it's over. I think we'll be OK.'

Tima nodded. Her network of insect and arachnid friends was sending a similar message; she was pretty sure the mammals were doing the same for Elena. She had grieved for the ants that had died for them, although a surprising number had survived their blast through the water. The fish and mammals and birds seem to have come through it all OK, too.

A wave of wonder and privilege swamped her whenever she thought about the allies they had.

She only wished that the Spin thing would sort itself out, so her friend could be happier. But if Spin really had been wiped, maybe it never would. Maybe Elena was mourning the boy she had known . . . because judging by what they'd seen in the park, Spin, as they had known him, was gone forever.

CHAPTER 54

The dark called to him. He sat up in bed and thought about going out. There was a place he wanted to go.

He just didn't know where it was.

He rose and dressed. His coat had been cleaned, dried, mended. It was good as new. There were no gadgets in the pockets; Astrid had removed them because most had been ruined by water. She hadn't asked what had happened. And he couldn't remember what they were for anyway, so he didn't ask either.

He shrugged the coat on over his black sweater, black jeans and black boots. Visions kept slashing through his mind, like three second movie trailers. A small dark-haired girl running across a park, screaming; a bird struggling in his hands; a gun on his neck; a tall chimney erupting into flame; fighting with a dark-haired boy; wasps swarming around his face; beautiful flowers crumbling to dust; water pouring through broken glass; a fair-haired girl sitting at a darkened window; framed like the Mona Lisa; the two girls with hot dogs in the park. He'd actually seen them, though . . . just a few days ago, out with Astrid. Were they connected?

He remembered the face of the fair-haired girl. Her expression had been frozen. She had looked like a marble statue as he walked past. Suddenly he saw her playing a trumpet against a red, glowering sky. It was official. Astrid was right. He was wrong in the head.

He slipped out of the house, liking the feeling of the coat and its red silk lining. He pressed his hands into his hair, pushing it back off his forehead, then unlocked the gate and eased himself into the woods.

It was a terraced street. He needed to go into the gardens at the back. But . . . where?

He stood, surrounded by trees, closing his eyes and waiting for the memory to stir in him again. He only saw the Mona Lisa girl. She was carrying rocks and dropping them on metal. There was blood on her face.

There was movement in the trees. A fox walked out into a small clearing, silvered by moonlight. It sat down, curled its tail around its paws, and gave him a look.

'What?' he asked it, in a surprisingly tetchy tone.

The fox stood up, turned, and walked away, tail held high. Then it paused, looked back at him, and moved its head in a jerk as if to say: 'Come on. *This* way, you idiot.'

With a growing sense of déjà vu, Spin followed it.

The house was dark. It was past 4 a.m. so that was no surprise. He stood in the modest back garden and stared at the patio. Another flash. A girl with a crucifix around her neck. He felt a dark surge of energy. His blood fizzed a little.

He shook his head, rubbing his hands across his face. He was living in a riddle.

'Spin?'

She walked out through the back door, stopping to casually stroke the head of the fox that had led him here. It was the Mona Lisa girl. He peered at her, curiously. She stepped closer, looking astonished . . . and a little wary.

He tried one of his happy smiles.

She winced. 'Oh no,' she said. 'Really . . . don't do that.'

'*Don't do what?*' he said.

She giggled, her hands over her mouth. Then she let them drop and shook her head. 'I'm sorry . . . it's . . . just not *you*.'

There it was again. *He wasn't himself.*

'What *is* me?' he asked.

'You . . .' she pointed to his hair, ' . . . usually wax this back, vampire style.'

'Vampire style?'

She held out her crucifix. 'There's a reason why I wear this.'

Her face, upturned in the moonlight, looked very nice. He felt another surge of energy. He stepped towards her . . . and felt a stabbing pain in his backside as the fox sank its teeth into him.

'Dammit, haven't you had *enough* of my blood?!' he snapped, twisting around to see the creature back away with a warning growl.

'Takes one to know one,' said the girl, folding her arms and looking smug.

'I do not bite people in the backside!' he said. 'I have a little more style than that!'

A light switched on in the upstairs bedroom, sending a shaft of gold across the garden and Elena's grinning face.

'You're back!' she whispered, before glancing worriedly up at the bedroom window. 'Oh Spin! I thought you'd been wiped forever . . . but you're back! Now . . . get out of here!'

CHAPTER 55

It was the last day of November; sunny and bright and she was alone in the park. An hour from now families would spill out across the swings and roundabout and slide, but not yet. Apart from a few pigeons she had it to herself.

She wasn't sure he would show up and part of her was afraid that if he did, he might come back again in his *Spin By Day* persona, grinning inanely.

But that was in the past now. As he walked through the gate and along the path, kicking up fallen leaves, he was wearing the usual black attire and the usual Spin swagger.

Two nights ago Velma had brought him to the garden because she knew her human friend was sad and it had to do with the pale boy—the one Velma had bitten once. Spin had gone seconds after Elena's mum woke up and started pulling the curtains open. But he'd returned the next night and spent twenty minutes talking to her. They hadn't had an all-out heart to heart. This was Spin, after all, back in full mind-messing mode. But they had shared some of the stuff that had happened at Thornleigh reservoir; as much as he could remember. She'd been able to thank him, too, for coming to help when he could have stayed safely away.

'I got you all into it,' he'd said, with a shrug. 'Had to make some effort to get you all out.'

Then they'd talked about his condition and the miracle of the blood exchange. It was working. He could be out in the sun without the usual agony. So she'd said: 'OK . . . meet me in the morning. At the park. At 9 a.m. I'd like to see you . . . the *actual* you . . . out in the day.'

And here he was.

When he got close enough he did a little turn on the spot, arms raised to the bright winter sky.

'See?' he said, blinking rapidly. 'I'm not on fire!'

She couldn't quite take in the strangeness. 'Does this mean you're not a vampire any more?'

'Did I ever say I was?' he asked, falling into step with her as she made for the swings.

'I don't think you needed to *say* it.'

He shrugged and rubbed his face. 'I never explain,' he said. 'If I can help it. I never apologize, either . . . in case you're still waiting.'

'I'm not waiting,' she said. 'Although if you *could* ever apologize to Matt, that would make our lives much easier. He should be ready to forgive you for all the fights by now.'

Spin sat on the swing next to hers and dropped his head. He seemed to be grinning. He didn't speak. What was going on in that odd brain of his?

'It must be weird for you, out in the day after so many years,' she said.

'Weird is one word for it,' he said, in a low voice. He glanced around at her and then looked down, staring at his hands. Was he . . . *blushing*? He was colouring up, no question. Elena had never, ever thought she would see Spin blush. He wasn't the kind to ever get embarrassed.

He was *shaking* too. He seemed like he was working up to telling her something . . . something important. She held her breath, waiting for him. And at last he lifted his head.

'I need to go,' he said.

'Spin?'

But now he was on his feet and his face was beetroot red. Was he *angry* with her? What had she done?

'This won't work,' said Spin. And without a further word he walked away, leaving her swaying to a shocked halt on the swings.

He didn't come back.

CHAPTER 56

He caught the bus. There wasn't enough tree cover to run. He got a wary look from the driver, with his cowl up over his head, but he paid his fare and made it to a seat at the back.

A shaft of light found his hand as they turned downtown. It was like a blowtorch.

So much for the Mayfly Cure. Months of life in watery gloom followed by just one glorious day in the sun ... then it was all over.

Astrid was waiting for him at the bus stop. It was as if she knew. She had a black golfing umbrella with her. Beneath it she was crying.

'I'm sorry,' she said. 'I'm so, so sorry.'

And he understood.

It came from her.

ACKNOWLEDGEMENTS

I could not have written this book without Sam and Claire Taylor. Sam is a great deal nicer than Spin, but he does share Spin's condition—Erythropoietic Protoporphyria.

At time of writing, Sam is just a little older than Spin and his guidance about what it's actually like to live with EPP, as a child and as a teenager, has been invaluable across Night Speakers and Night Raiders—but especially in Night Walker with the emergence of Spin's back story.

Sam's mum Claire, like Astrid, is also an EPP sufferer and her insights have been vital. She doesn't throw roundhouse kicks at Sam without warning, though (as far as I know). In fact they're both fantastic people managing something really tough and endlessly painful with currently little hope of a cure—and I salute them for their dignity and humour.

The BPA put me in touch with Claire and Sam, so I owe the association a huge debt of thanks too. (*And ask forgiveness for the vampire thing!*)

Although elements of Spin's condition have been *very slightly* heightened for the story, it's all extremely close to reality for an EPP sufferer.

Living in shadow can be incredibly hard and the treatments even harder. The blood cell exchange is every bit as brutal as Spin's experience and currently offers only a temporary respite.

EPP is a very rare condition and, like any rare condition, doesn't get much attention or research funding. If you are interesting in helping out in any way, please do contact the British Porphyria Association at **www.porphyria.org.uk**.

Ali Sparkes, April 2019

ALI SPARKES

Ali Sparkes was a journalist and BBC broadcaster until she chucked in the safe job to go dangerously freelance and try her hand at writing comedy scripts. Her first venture was as a comedy columnist on *Woman's Hour* and later on *Home Truths*. Not long after, she discovered her real love was writing children's fiction.

Ali grew up adoring adventure stories about kids who mess about in the woods and still likes to mess about in the woods herself whenever possible. She lives with her husband and two sons in Southampton, England.

HAVE YOU READ
THEM ALL?

THE SHAPESHIFTER